# My

# Son

# The

# Enemy

by

# David Hughes

*My Son The Enemy*

**Published and Printed by**

Papercraft, Unit 5-6, Crowther Industrial Estate, Washington, Tyne & Wear NE38 0AD Tel: 0191 415 7100

**Promoted by**

Chester-le-Street Rotary Club - (Charitable Trust)

*All profits to be jointly shared between*

"Help for Heroes" & "The Army Benevolent Fund"

# The Rotary Club of Chester-le-Street

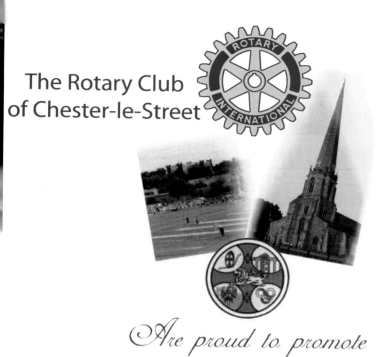

*Are proud to promote*

## "My Son The Enemy"

*by*

*Rotarian David Hughes*

*all profits will be jointly donated to...*

www.chester-le-streetrotary.co.uk

My Son The Enemy

This book is dedicated

to

Bill Fish

No man could have had a better friend

# Acknowledgements

### Naval Advisor

Sub Lieutenant R.N.V.R. (Retired)

John Parkinson

### Military Advisor

Warrant Officer – (Retired) Special

Investigation Branch, Royal Military Police)

Kevin Jobson

### Proof Reader

Mrs Beryl Pratt

# Special Acknowledgement To A Friend

Mrs Ruby Neil is a 79 year old retired secretary, who has been married 52 years, and has four children and five grandchildren.

Over a period of many months she has deciphered my poor handwriting, corrected my atrocious spelling and tolerated my continuous editing and re-writing without losing her smile or enthusiasm.

# Foreword

by

### Colonel Alex K. Johnson  M.B.E. T.D. Minst.Re.DL.

On reading the first chapter – The Forgotten War – I thought it was going to be another history book, then I realised it was purely a background to a historical novel – WHAT A BACKGROUND!!

I was serving in the Army in 1946, but I had no idea what was happening in Palestine and Cyprus. This chapter has completed my education in that area and I am duly grateful.

The portrayal of the Weisman family was excellent, and the story of Lieut. Allan Lambert was life-like and handled with great delicacy.

Having been in Belsen at the takeover I have great admiration for the Author's description of the Camps, and the unfortunate inmates.

I was proud that we British had released them, but having read this book I now have mixed feelings about our part in the episode.

The love aspect of the story was treated with dignity, gradually working up to a wonderful ending.

I read the story three times and I grew to like it more each time. The Author should be congratulated on a fine piece of writing.

**ARMY BENEVOLENT FUND**
**THE SOLDIERS' CHARITY**

**SUPPORTING THOSE**
**WHO DEFEND YOU**

**www.armybenfund.org**

*Soldiers are a proud bunch. It takes a lot for them to ask for help, but sometimes the need is so great that they simply cannot manage on bravery alone.*

**The Army Benevolent Fund is the Soldiers' Charity**

Since the end of the Second World War the Fund has given financial support and practical advice to soldiers, former soldiers and their families when they find themselves in real need. The principle the charity works to is that a 'hand up' is better than a 'hand out'.

**How and who we help**

Around half the money the charity raises each year is given directly to support individuals in partnership with the Regimental or Corps Benevolent Fund. The need can take many form's, examples are an electric wheelchair, stair lift, care home fees or adapting the home of a soldier to enable him to cope with two children suffering from cerebral palsy. The rest of the money the charity raises is given to support some 80 other charities that look after the special needs of the Army Family. These include The Army Families Federation, the British Limbless Ex-Servicemen's Association, Combat Stress and the 'Not Forgotten Association

**Why we need you support**

Dependant on voluntary donations, the Fund must currently raise over £5.5 million each year to continue its vital work to support the Army Family. The need will not abate for many years, indeed it will increase as costs continue to rise.

*The Army Benevolent Fund is the Principal Charity for the British Army. It has supported the Army Family for over 65 years, it is in it for the long haul and will be around as long as the need exists.*

**www.armybenfund.org**

# The Forgotten War
## by David Hughes

Every year we remember war exploits from World War One, World War Two, Iraq, Northern Ireland, to the Falklands, yet a conflict involving almost 90,000 British soldiers, almost 800 deaths, and an unknown number of incidents including hangings, beatings and other atrocities is virtually unknown by many British citizens. Associated with this carnage was the treatment inflicted on Jewish Holocaust survivors in the name of the British government.

Not only is this slice of history ignored today, reporting was curtailed at the time and practically all evidence has been obliterated. It is as if it never happened, but it did, and I was there.

The year was 1946, World War Two had ended, Nazi concentration camps in Europe had been opened and survivors were released after six years of horror. Thousands headed for Palestine 'The Promised Land' with the hope to begin a new life.

Large ships, rusty old boats, anything that could float and survive the journey across the Mediterranean Sea, were utilised. Jews of many nationalities were heading for a land where they were wanted, needed and would be free from further persecution.

However, their freedom would last only for the length of their sea journey, when they would be returned to captivity by the British.

Palestine had been under the control of the British since the end of World War One when Jews were in the minority, lived in Ghettos and in relative harmony with the Arab majority.

Hitler's persecution of the Jews resulted in a mass migration of Jews from Europe into Palestine with the result that the population balance changed. The Jews became more dominant, wealthy and more ambitious than their Arab neighbours. No longer a small minority, the Jews wanted a piece of Palestine for themselves.

They ruthlessly pursued their demands with the assistance of two terrorist gangs, the 'Stern' and the 'Urgun'. By 1946 the fighting in Palestine was horrific, with Jews fighting Arabs and the British Army in the middle of the two. There was no limit to the atrocities. The killing was unrelenting with the British Paratroop Regiments taking major casualties, the King David Hotel was bombed, British soldiers hanged in the street and a village was attacked by the Jews to *"teach the Arabs a lesson".* Men, women and children were slaughtered. Jews were killing Arabs, Arabs killing Jews with British casualties escalating at an alarming rate.

Because of all the turmoil, Britain decided that the mass exodus of concentration camp survivors would not be allowed to land on Palestinian soil.

A naval force including 'Chieftain', 'Chequers', and 'Magpie' diverted the old ships to Famagusta Harbour on the island of Cyprus. Helmeted navy sailors using shields, batons and water cannon easily stopped any attempt to avoid further captivity by concentration camp survivors.

Many of the traumatised Jews were still suffering from their treatment by the Nazis and were unable to comprehend how their British liberators were now the enemy. A few young men put up a fight, but a cracked skull quelled any uprising, and the majority simply succumbed to their fate. Any medical or mental progress they had made during their sea voyage was eliminated. The trauma and shock was catastrophic. Those on the verge of mental instability were pushed to the edge, panic attacks escalated and a blanket of gloom descended like a shroud. A few jumped overboard in a vain attempt to escape and those near death – died.

Their arrival at Famagusta brought back frightening memories, as they faced a fortress of armed soldiers and were forced to disembark. The harbour was engulfed in an eerie silence, and even the soldiers were shocked to see a slow line of haggard skeletons heading for the trucks with an occasional sob, a child's cry and a yell when an attempt to escape was thwarted.

Their first sight of the camp at 'Karaolus', north of Famagusta harbour was even more traumatic. German prisoners of war had built the camp, which was surrounded by a high barbed wire fence, gun turrets and search lights. Many survivors were convinced they had simply changed six years of German persecution for an unknown period of British captivity.

Over the next two years, more than 50,000 holocaust survivors were held captive in camps in Cyprus, all being guarded and controlled by British troops. They were fed, clothed and given medical treatment, but freedom outside the barbed wire fence was denied.

As time passed the health of the inmates improved, they created their own activities and environment within the camps, but security was so tight a successful escape attempt was rare.

Although they were not subject to the horrors of their previous German captors, every face behind the barbed wire fence was etched with hatred and loathing for their British guards.

In May 1948 the State of Israel was declared. Many Arab families living on the wrong side of the new boundary became refugees. Camps on Cyprus were closed, survivors were finally allowed into their 'Promised Land' and British soldiers were withdrawn.

One of the first decrees by the Jewish Terrorists was to declare that no British soldier with the rank of Sergeant and above would ever be allowed on Israel soil.

Seeds of hatred were sown at the end of World War Two. For more than sixty years violence has escalated and widened to a degree no one could have imagined. The hatred by the Palestinians against the Jews for taking their land is so intense it may never be eradicated. Jews will never allow criticism, opposition or questioning of their right to their own State and over the years Britain's attempts at conciliation have been less than successful.

Little did I realise during my involvement in 1946 that Jews and Palestinians would still be fighting sixty years later.

*This story, although fictional,*

*is inspired by actual events*

# Contents

# *Introduction*

Millions of words have been written concerning the horror of the holocaust, survivors, perpetrators and historians have all made tremendous contributions that will far outweigh my submission to a subject that is full of contention. Having read volumes on the subject, spoken to many people involved and being able to speak with personal experience on a part of this story, I have attempted to encapsulate the atrocities of so called civilised people into an exercise of fiction.

I have created one family who were all touched in varying degrees by appalling acts of violence against innocent people. Some incidents were motivated by a state, others the sheer brutality of individuals.

This is not an exercise in chronological history, nor is it a repetition of holocaust testimonies, it is a work of fiction that shows how all members of one Jewish family suffered through the actions of Germans, Palestinians, British and by other Jews.

Many incidents are based on truth.

# The Weisman Family

---

## Isaac Weisman born 1875

## Irene Weisman born 1880

---

❋   ❋   ❋   ❋

| SARAH born 1901 | ALBERT born 1902 | IRENE born 1904 |
|---|---|---|
| married | married | married |
| Sir John Lambert b.1881 | Hannah born 1904 | David Schuman died 1925 |
| | (2 daughters) | (Son Simon) born 1925 |

❋   ❋   ❋   ❋

The Weismans were a close family unit, very affluent, living in a mansion in the centre of a vibrant Jewish community in Berlin, Germany. Their jewellery empire had been in the family for three generations and son, Albert, was expected to take the business into the fourth generation when his father retired.

It was a loving family with a pampered life style that opulent wealth can provide. They had no experience of the desires and needs of the average German citizen, hardship, hunger and deprivation were outside their orbit of life. However the family were generous to any genuine charity appeal and were held in high esteem within their community.

The inevitable jealousy existed, particularly among the non-Jewish residents of Berlin and when the opportunity arose, bitterness and anger were released to a degree of incredible proportions and the Weisman family had more to lose and further to fall than anyone else in the community.

# Chapter One
# A Sinister Note

*"Good God, what's wrong?"*

Lieutenant Harry Arnold watched his fellow officer turn white, slump down into his chair, beads of sweat appearing on his forehead. Allan Lambert didn't reply, he just stared at the piece of paper the young waiter had quietly slipped into his hand together with his change.

*"Let me see that."* Harry leaned forward with his hand outstretched, but Allan quickly put the paper into the top pocket of his uniform jacket, gave Harry a mumbled apology and quickly walked out of the restaurant.

Harry's eyes followed his friend's departure with disbelief, this was so unusual. They had known each other for almost three years, had always been open and straight with each other, but this must be serious. Harry could only sit still and finish off their bottle of Commanderia wine, it was too good to waste.

They were both junior officers in the British Army stationed in Famagusta on the island of Cyprus, the year was 1946 and they had been posted to the Middle East to be part of a special task unit whose activity would one day be subjected to worldwide publicity, criticism and condemnation.

From the day they were commissioned at Budbrook Barracks in Warwickshire, England, the two twenty one year olds had become as close as brothers, not in looks, but their temperament, humour and love of tall slim blondes was identical. Harry was dark skinned, five foot six inches tall with thick black curly hair and a permanent smile, he'd been brought up in Cardiff, the middle son of five brothers. He'd escaped from the slums by joining the army as a boy soldier and was now one of the few black officers in the British Army overseas, he'd endured racial abuse and intimidation on his slow elevation to the rank of Lieutenant.

Allan Lambert was tall, blonde, with his father's blue eyes, a typical English army officer, he was straight as a ramrod with an immaculate public school accent, occasionally he displayed a short temper, but basically was a friendly and likeable young officer who was destined for future promotion, mainly because he had the right connections.

They had opposite backgrounds, but in the past three years had cemented a deep friendship that seemed unbreakable.

However, Harry Arnold would have been angry and devastated had he been aware of the true identity of his friend.

Allan Lambert was not an Englishman, he was a German by birth and to further complicate his situation he was a German Jew, with false identity papers, serving in the British Army at a time of hostilities.

Although World War Two with Germany had been won, the bitter fighting with Jews in Palestine still continued with British soldiers being killed every day.

Allan and Harry had been posted to Cyprus to deal with Jewish holocaust survivors. They were responsible for controlling stores full of bedding, clothing etc and were on daily standby awaiting the first ship full of Jewish survivors from Nazi concentration camps that would be escorted into Famagusta Harbour by the British navy.

Once a week they both enjoyed the luxury of a night out on the town with a good meal and a bottle of wine, afterwards they always parted company. Harry's black skin seemed to be less attractive to the blondes, so he made a weekly visit to the brothel while Allan returned to the officers' mess to try his luck with the half dozen Wrens who were

2

regular guests.

This night Allan had no thought for blondes, Wrens or the officers' mess, he returned to his room as fast as he could, locked the door, switched on the light and slumped into a chair. He took the piece of paper from his pocket and looked at it long and hard, over and over he read the words, past memories and foreboding crowding his thoughts. Everything in his life was suddenly at risk, career, friends, even his freedom, *"God Almighty"*, he thought aloud, *"Susan, she'd never marry him now".* Knowledge of his real identity would be the end, her father hated Jews with a passion, having recently retired as a chief inspector in the Palestine police force, and Susan would never defy her father.

The writing was almost a blur by the time Allan put the piece of paper safely into his pocket, he slowly undressed, climbed into bed, pulling the blanket over his head in an attempt to block out the world, but sleep wouldn't come, he'd never felt so troubled.

------ o ------

*"You look bloody awful!"* Harry Arnold greeted his friend next morning at breakfast. *"Just what the hell's wrong, can I help?"*

Allan Lambert didn't lift his head from his untouched breakfast and quietly replied, *"Harry, I'm so sorry, one day I'll explain, you may even be able to help, but please, not now."*

Harry realised he shouldn't interfere.

*"I'm here whenever you need me, what's your immediate plans?"*

Allan lifted his eyes, looked at his friend and said, *"I'm off duty today, I'm going up to Salamis to be on my own and think."*

*"It's that bloody note you were given last night isn't it?*

Allan didn't answer, he slowly rose to his feet, *"See you later, keep out of trouble."*

He walked from the officers' mess without turning or acknowledging

3

morning greetings from fellow officers.

After signing out of the Depot at the Guard House he picked up the keys for his jeep and with screeching tyres Allan drove out of the camp on to the Salamis road.

It was 9 a.m. on a beautiful morning in March, the only traffic on the narrow road was the occasional army lorry throwing up clouds of dust and the occasional Cypriot with his little donkey cart clipping along the road.  Allan took very little notice of them or the fields full of grapes, melons and tomatoes, they were a regular sight on the island to which he'd become accustomed.  However the stark and empty internment camps were more disturbing with their high barbed wire fences, gun turrets and searchlights.

*"The Jews won't be happy at being forced to enter such dismal surroundings after six years in German concentration camps,"* Allan silently mused, but he had enough of his own problems to worry about.

He didn't stop until he arrived at the one place in Cyprus that gave him perfect peace, his friends preferred to visit the mountains of Troodos, or the quiet town of Larnaca, for Allan, the ruins of Salamis were his haven.

He parked his jeep and with a feeling of near reverence, sat down on the nearest boulder and drank in the pure splendour. To the uninitiated he was sitting on a pile of stones, but Allan was aware that he was in the midst of the once great city of Salamis, he looked out at acres of majestic columns that were now broken, jagged and forlorn, he was sitting on the very spot where a vibrant Greek forum once stood, but his surroundings were as dead as he felt.

As the smoke from his cigarette curled upwards in the calm atmosphere, the only sound was from the multitude of birds and insects. Taking off his army jacket, Allan slowly walked up the broken steps of the amphitheatre, at the summit he turned and viewed the expanse of the ancient forum and tried to make sense of his predicament.

Allan knew that he looked like a typical English army officer, tall, lean and erect, his sun tan enhanced his features, he even thought of himself as English, his fellow officers had no doubt, but he knew that his heritage had no English or even Christian connections, he was a German and a Jew with false identity papers.

Into his second cigarette, Allan allowed his thoughts to drift back to his childhood and the last time he'd seen his dear mother.

A crowded railway station in Berlin, the year was 1930, he was five years old, his name was Simon Schuman and he was in the centre of a group that included his grandparents, aunt, uncle and his dear mother. He could not understand why they were all so tearful, his mother had given him a tight hug and with tears streaming down her face whispered, *"It won't be for long, my darling, you enjoy your holiday in England with Aunt Sarah, I'll see you soon, always remember I love you."*

His uncle Albert had gently eased him away from his mother, walked him along the busy platform to a tall bearded man with the words, *"Be a good boy."*

Then with tears streaming down his face his uncle handed him and his small suitcase over to the stranger, turned and almost ran back down the platform. Allan remembered screaming for his mother, tried to tear himself from the stranger, but within seconds he was bundled on to a train just as it pulled out of the station. He clearly remembered feeling hysterical as he cowered in the corner of the carriage and being overwhelmed by distress and disbelief, but sleep mercifully calmed his sobbing little body.

He woke up to see this strange man doing all he could to be friendly, he had food and drink, a huge smile and words of reassurance that his holiday in England would be wonderful then he'd return home.

With help from the man he began to enjoy looking out of the carriage window interested in the passing scene, taking his mind away from leaving his mother. After two days of travel they had landed at Dover and then he was delivered to his aunt Sarah at a luxury apartment in Kensington, London.

His Aunt Sarah immediately reminded him of his mother, she had black hair, a kind smiling face and she cuddled him tight with assurance that he'd be alright.

The tall man who said he was *'Uncle John'* had a harsh unfriendly voice, and seemed to be very unhappy with Aunt Sarah. Simon couldn't understand their language and it had taken him a long time to settle down in the home of his aunt.

If only his holiday could end and he could see his mother and grandparents again, he was so homesick he cried himself to sleep every night, everything in his life was so different – he was utterly miserable.

Allan Lambert sat alone at Salamis with tears streaming down his face, remembering those days as they were yesterday. However, sixteen years had passed and so much had happened to him, he had never been allowed to return to Berlin, and had no idea the fate his family had suffered.

He now had a new identity, no longer called Simon Schuman and living the life of a Christian English army officer.

Everything in his life was false.

# Chapter Two

# Early Signs Of Trouble

Simon Schuman, (now Allan Lambert) had been born in Berlin, Germany on December 19th 1925 at the imposing detached mansion of his grandparents, Isaac and Irene Weisman, the baby's mother Irene having become a widow only three months prior to the birth. The baby's father, David Schuman, an Austrian mountain climber, had died suddenly from a heart attack while on an expedition in Switzerland.

David combined his love of mountaineering with his work as a lawyer. He had met Irene on a skiing holiday in Austria. It was love at first sight and although not of the Jewish faith her parents accepted him with a warmth and genuine affection. Recently he had completed some legal work for his father-in-law. Irene was expecting their first child, but a massive heart attack confirmed his doctor's warning six months prior that he should "slow down".

The baby's grandparents had installed their youngest daughter into an apartment within their mansion until the baby was born, after which she could decide on her future plans.

Tired after a long, but uncomplicated delivery of her first baby, Irene Schuman had been attended by two specialist doctors and the family nurse, the boy was ten pounds in weight with blonde curly hair like his father. All that money could buy had been and would continue to be lavished on mother and child, they had been deprived of a kind, gentle father and Irene knew that no one would ever match up to her beloved husband for as long as she lived. The atmosphere throughout the house had been of relief, elation and uncontrolled joy, the baby had joined their world of affluence and contentment.

The baby's grandfather, Isaac Weisman, was a German and proud of it, he had many German friends and had built up a highly successful jewellery business with shops throughout Germany. He was a very wealthy man with a loving wife and a delightful family of a son and two daughters, and now his third grandchild had arrived, Isaac was a contented man.

The high unemployment and recent riots throughout Germany were cause for some concern and not good for business, but Isaac had seen it all before, he felt sure he could ride another storm, although the stories about the upstart called Adolf Hitler was a slight worry, everyone trying to get attention in politics always targeted the Jews at some time. There had always been people in Germany who were envious of the Jews, but Isaac had found that wealth could calm many situations if it was distributed wisely. He had learned how to insulate his family from intimidation, so he had no fears for the recent stories circulating from Berlin.

Isaac had seen Jewish intimidation all his life. His family had always lived in Berlin and after inheriting his father's small jewellery shop he had built it into an empire. As his wealth grew he realised he could isolate his family from bullying, intimidation and fear by paying the right people to ensure safety. He saw no problem in paying Germans to give him peace of mind against politically motivated thugs.

He tried to calm hysterical friends at the synagogue but was often rebuffed with comments such as,

*"You can buy your way out of troubles"*! or *"You can emigrate any time you wish"*!

*"This is my country, I'm not leaving for anyone"*! was Isaac's constant retort.

No matter who controlled Germany, Isaac Weisman firmly believed that his wealth, position in the community and loyalty to his beloved Germany would shield him and his family from any potential troubles.

*"I'm going to the synagogue to give thanks for my new grandson,"* Isaac said to his wife as he fixed his homberg hat firmly on to his head. Rolled umbrella in his hand, he then strolled down the avenue with the full knowledge that he was a highly respected pillar of the Jewish community, help and support he never refused and his name was spoken with reverence.

Outside the synagogue his dearest friend was sitting on a bench seat waiting to greet him with the warm words, *"Congratulations on the new addition to your family Isaac!"*

*"Thank you Abel, I am indeed a fortunate man with a wonderful family,"* Isaac replied, a genuine smile on his face.

*"Can you give me a moment of your time?"*

*"Of course",* Isaac replied, *"Give me ten minutes and I'll meet you here."*

The two men sat on their favourite seat outside the synagogue, enjoying the neat, tidy garden, the air was crisp, and the bird song broke the silence.

*"I'm going, Isaac!"* Abel blurted out the words as if to be rid of them as quickly as possible, Isaac didn't reply, they had been there for each other in good and bad times, their families had grown up together, distance wouldn't break their fifty years bond of friendship.

*"Why don't you get out with us, my dear friend?"* Abel turned with pleading eyes, but immediately recognised the set face of rejection, a reply wasn't really necessary from Isaac.

*"I wish you and your family well, Abel, you've talked about this for a long time, so you've finally made up your mind!"*

They both stood, gave each other a hug and a firm handshake, Isaac looked long and hard into the eyes of the man he loved as a brother. *"Let me know when you and your family arrive safely in America."* Isaac turned away quickly before Abel could see the tears in his eyes, then he walked slowly home with a greater sadness than he'd ever felt.

His friend had joined the exodus of Jews from Germany. Returning home, he gave his wife the sad news and she took the opportunity to say, *"Could you please consider our family emigrating? So many of our friends have gone, we could even go to England, Sarah would love to see us safe over there".*

*"Irene, we are Germans and we are not running away!",* they had had the same conversation time and again, but even his beloved wife couldn't influence Isaac to leave the country of his birth and the business he had built into a financial empire.

In spite of the stories and rumours about the intimidation and beating of Jews, Isaac had seen nothing and stubbornly considered himself and his family to be immune from the terror his friends forecast.

Over the next few years Isaac felt vindicated, the economic situation in Germany improved, inflation was lower, and everyone had a more contented outlook for the future. Isaac's new grandson, Simon, was his pride and joy and growing into a beautiful boy, business was booming and Isaac fully expected some of his friends to return to Germany. Even the 1928 election in Germany was cause for some optimism although Hitler's brown shirted stormtroopers marched through Berlin, saluted their leader and called him 'Fuhrer', his party received only 2% of the votes.

Sadly the Wall Street crash was the beginning of the catastrophe, Germany was the worst hit country, five banks crashed and in 1931 the world was swept into economic disaster. The high unemployment, misery and hunger persuaded the people of Germany to listen to

Adolf Hitler, he spoke at rallies throughout the country, promised to solve the economic problems and make Germany great once again, as it had been prior to World War One. He was received with wild enthusiasm, little did the German people realise the path down which he would lead them.

Isaac Weisman and six million Jews were doomed.

# My Son The Enemy

# Chapter Three

## Looking For A Husband

Baby Simon had been three months old when his aunt Sarah went on holiday to England in 1926, all the family knew that Sarah was becoming desperate for marriage with a dread of being an old maid, she didn't have the typical features of a Jewess, considered herself to be attractive with a wealthy family background. She had had several boy friends, all good Jewish boys whose parents had manipulated the friendships with the hope that money would never be a problem if their son could marry into the Weisman fortune. However Sarah had ambitions far greater than any local Jewish boy could provide, she wanted challenge, status, and excitement in her life. Now she was twenty five years old and on a visit to England, a country she'd looked forward to visiting for a long time, it may just provide a suitable husband.

Installed in the fashionable Waldorf Hotel in London with ample connections provided by her father, Sarah began to explore the social demands of the city's high society. During the day she was taken to the British Museum and other London treasures and in the evenings if not at a West End theatre she was invited to a party, London had never ending parties in the mid 1920s.

After five weeks her constant round of parties was becoming a bore, the same people making the same small talk, drinking too much and pretending to be happy. Sarah was no nearer to being a married woman and decided to return to Germany within a week, but she agreed to accept one more party invitation at the famous Savoy hotel.

There was the usual elegant splendour and small talk with the same partygoers, when mid-way through the evening she heard the voice of Peter Hauxwell her evening chaperone, who was well aware of her desire to become a married woman, say, *"Sir John, can I introduce you to my friend from Germany, Miss Sarah Weisman?"*

Sarah turned to see a tall, slim, erect gentleman in an immaculate tailored evening suit adorned by a red carnation and a charming smile on his face that displayed perfect white teeth.

*"Sarah, this is Sir John Lambert from the Foreign Office".*

It was not love at first sight, he was charming and more interesting than the usual partygoers, but Sarah did not have the impression that he could be her knight in shining armour ready to whisk her to marriage and life long happiness, he may even be married, but he was interesting, good looking, and aged maybe in his early forties.

John Lambert was, in fact, forty six years old and Sarah would have been shocked had she been aware of his thoughts the moment he turned. Sarah had a fabulous figure draped in a gown that shouted wealth, stunning looks and long straight black hair, he immediately thought she would be the perfect adornment on his arm at official functions. Her name Weisman was obviously Jewish but she didn't look like a Jew, and at her age she may be looking for a husband.

John Lambert devoted the remainder of the evening to Sarah, displayed his wealth of knowledge, charm and well cultivated charisma, he sowed the seeds in Sarah's mind that he may be the one, particularly when he disclosed that he had never been married and any future wife of his would acquire the title of *'Lady'.*

In the high echelons of the civil service he was aware that a wife was an asset, almost an essential for future promotion or honours, Sarah

Weisman would be ideal, she was a Jew and he hated Jews, but he considered that she would be accepted in society particularly when she had the title of 'Lady Lambert'. He was confident he would be able to change her attitude to her Jewish faith, in return for the high life in London.

To Sarah, his friends and colleagues, Sir John Lambert appeared to be the perfect English gentleman, he was courteous, immaculately dressed and always walked the short distance to his office with his perfectly rolled umbrella, homburg hat and a neatly folded newspaper under his arm.

However, this pillar of society was neither a gentleman nor an Englishman, he was born in 1881 in the slums of Dublin, Ireland during the famine. He was an only child, his mother, Mary, was unable to bear more than the one child and he was named Patrick (Connelly) after his unemployed alcoholic father. At the age of two years Patrick had travelled with his family to the East End of London with high hopes of a better living, they settled in a slum area dominated by Jews who hated the Irish interlopers.

Patrick's father had plans to improve their situation, but drink always delayed his ambition and everyone knew that the police would one day catch up with his thieving.

For as long as he could remember the young boy had vowed to himself that one day when he was older he would escape from the slums of London's East End and be rid of his Jewish tormentors for ever.

His opportunity came when he was only twelve years old when an epidemic of tuberculosis swept through the slums killing Jews, Gentiles and his father, followed by the demise of his dear mother within three months. His Jewish neighbours gave neither care, comfort nor sympathy to the orphaned young boy, although one old lady did give him the address of an orphanage four miles away.

He knocked on the door and pleaded to be admitted, told the nun who interviewed him that he could not find any identification papers after his parents died because everything they owned had been stolen from him. He claimed that his name was John Lambert (a name he had seen on a brass plate outside a house) and although his English name did not match his Irish accent, his pleading performance was masterful. The astute old nun realised that the young boy could be helpful with the younger children in return for taking him in and providing food and shelter.

Harold Hall was sixty years old, homeless and destitute when the nuns of St Francis agreed to give him food and shelter in exchange for his work in the orphanage as an odd job man, in the past ten years he had become indispensable, he was a well educated ex-teacher who had allowed drink to ruin his life, the young John Lambert was like a shining beacon in the eyes of Harold Hall who saw enthusiasm, ambition, energy and a spirit of determination that matched his own many years ago.

For the reformed alcoholic it was a new lease of life when the young John Lambert arrived. Harold now had a purpose for living, his knowledge and skill could be passed to a boy he would care for as if he was his son.

When Harold died eight years later he had helped to transform the young John Lambert into an educated English man. Gone was the Irish accent, he was now a smart, confident young man who had acquired a place at a minor university to the delight of the nuns and Mother Superior. He had made himself almost indispensable at the orphanage fully justifying their decision to accept him years earlier and now he was their pride and joy and an example to other orphans.

University was the perfect environment for the ambitious John Lambert, he did not mind admitting to anyone that he was an orphan who could not remember his childhood, it seemed to add a mystery to his image that suited his plans, he was determined to succeed at university and emerge as an English gentleman. By pure chance he discovered the illegal homosexual activities of a senior tutor and the son of a Lord, disclosure of such actions could result in disgrace, dishonour and possible imprisonment for the two people. They would give anything for their secret to be maintained and John Lambert had no sympathy or limits to his blackmailing demands.

The young student introduced him to all the right groups, organisations and associations that would otherwise be unavailable to someone with no connections and everyone assumed that they were close friends with impeccable family ties. The tutor was in desperation to safeguard his reputation and ensure the silence of his blackmailer, consequently, John Lambert received ample tuition, prior notification of examination questions and a Degree in Literature that had never been in doubt. His acceptance into the Civil Service ended his blackmailing activities and confirmed his achievement in reaching the pinnacle of his ambition to be accepted in high society as an English gentleman.

# My Son The Enemy

# *Chapter Four*
# *A Young Refugee*

The initial respect by Sarah Weisman for Sir John Lambert soon turned to a feeling of flattery, love and eventual passion, she was prepared to do anything, go anywhere and could not wait to be introduced as *'Lady Sarah Lambert'.*

John Lambert had made steady progress in the Civil Service, made himself indispensable and been rewarded with a knighthood, but his methods in acquiring power had created enemies who would delight in his downfall. A wife was almost a required asset and he realised that Sarah could be the ideal partner for his numerous social occasions, he had no doubt he could mould her to look and act the part of an English lady, he planned the pursuit of Sarah Weisman relentlessly.

Sir John did not ignore protocol, he visited Berlin regularly, met Sarah's parents and mentally calculated the dowry his future wife would produce. He avoided inviting her parents to England and their wedding ceremony took place in Berlin on May 7th 1927, well away from his colleagues, no one would know that his in-laws were Jews.

The age difference between the happy couple was ignored, the Weisman family were delighted to see their daughter wed to a 'Sir' and the 'Sir' was confident that a wife would be an asset, particularly the daughter of a wealthy jeweller.

After the wedding they both agreed that to have family at their age would not be practical. Little did Sarah know that her husband had no intention of fathering a child to a Jewish wife. Nor did Sir John know that a young Jewish refugee from Berlin would one day bring him humiliation and the disintegration of the image he had so carefully created over the past forty years.

However, Sarah was so in love she accepted everything John demanded, parties, dinners, anything that would further her husband's career, he was charming, attentive and affectionate, but when the door closed on their return home, he always left her on her own claiming he had work to complete.

Lady Sarah soon realised that Sir John had no love for her, his job and image were his only concern, he was self-opinionated, greedy and a bully, he banned her from attending the synagogue and refused any discussion on her Jewish faith or family in Berlin.

Eventually love, respect, even communication disappeared, Sarah was bitterly ashamed that she had allowed herself to forsake her religion, family and self respect in exchange for a husband and the title 'Lady Sarah Lambert'. The glamour of attending state functions, and the benefit from being 'Your Ladyship' had long faded, she hated herself for allowing John to mould her image and attitude into acting as a typical English lady.

After five years of marriage she hated her husband with a passion, she refused to attend official functions, claiming she had a permanent headache, they now shared only breakfast together – never a bed.

She longed to leave him and return to her parents in Berlin, but letters from her father pleaded that "she should stay in England until someone put a stop to the mad man, Adolf Hitler". Sarah was trapped in England, lonely, unhappy, with very few friends.

Unknown to her husband, Sarah had secretly made contact with the Rabbi of the local Synagogue, Rabbi Sackman encouraged her to confide in him and unburden her soul, make secret visits to the Synagogue and re-kindle her faith. He kept her up-to-date with the latest news from Germany, she divulged secrets and deceptions by her husband that should not have been aired but she was only too pleased to have such a friend.

Sarah would have been dismayed had she been aware that the Rabbi was an integral link in the chain of contacts of an underground movement that was rescuing as many Jews as possible from Germany. Her husband was now a senior figure in the Foreign Office, he hated Jews and would have been incensed with anger had he known of his wife's secret, particularly had he known that the Rabbi's main clandestine activity was his direct link with a Jewish Terrorist Group in Palestine called 'THE STERN GANG'.

The Rabbi had been ordered to cultivate the trust of Lady Lambert because of her husband, any information concerning his secrets or deceptions may be valuable to 'STERN' in future negotiations.

In 1932 many members of the British Government had the same anti-semitic views as Sir John Lambert, and acted to stop Jews emigrating to England, Sir John was more vocal than many of his colleagues in demanding a stop to the flood of Jews fleeing Germany, for him to help even one Jew to escape was unthinkable.

The Rabbi was instructed to make contact with Lady Sarah's family in Berlin and suggest they send the youngest member of the family to England for safety before the situation for Jews became worse.

After hours of family discussion, heartache, and streaming tears the young Simon's mother agreed that it would be for her son's safety that he be sent on a holiday to her sister Sarah in London, England, she was torn between emigrating with her son or staying in Berlin with her ageing parents. Her father was positive in his opinion that the problem with Hitler would not effect the family and business but Irene was persuaded by the whole family to send her Simon for a short holiday to England to his aunt and uncle, if the Rabbi could make the travel arrangements out of Berlin. The Schuman family had no idea that the husband of Sarah hated Jews.

*"Of course, I'd love to have Simon stay with us!"* Lady Sarah responded with joy in her voice when Rabbi Sackman returned to England and suggested the idea, but she immediately sank into a feeling of dismay at the thought of asking John such a favour. To the outside world, he had no love or contact with Jews and to get him to openly accept a young Jewish refugee from Berlin into his home was unthinkable.

She didn't sleep that night wondering how to approach her husband next morning and get his approval to accept her nephew for a holiday that may last for a long, long time.

With trepidation she sat down at breakfast, her *"Good morning"* was answered by his usual grunt without a lift of his eyes from his morning newspaper.

*"John, put your paper down, I have something serious to talk about."* With surprise at this sudden temerity in using such a tone of voice when speaking to him, Sir John slowly lowered his newspaper, stared at Sarah over the top of his reading glasses, never uttered a word and waited.

*"You know I have a young nephew in Berlin and the family are desperate to get him out of the country until the troubles with the Nazis blows over?"*

Sarah knew that her voice was trembling, her heart pounding and John just looking at her without any sign of emotion. She continued her well rehearsed speech, with some pleading in her voice, *"John, if you will do this for me I will support you at every function, organise your dinner parties and help you in every way I can, but please save little Simon."* She ended her pleading knowing that tears were flowing down her cheeks and she was silently sobbing.

Sir John made no comment, continued with his breakfast while his wife sat staring directly at him waiting for his response.

John was well aware that people were beginning to question his wife's absence from Foreign Office functions, his excuses were wearing thin and he would be only too pleased to have her by his side once again in order to maintain his image of having a happy marriage and an attentive wife. Taking in a young Jewish brat could be easily managed with his influences and connections, to Sarah he simply broke his silence by saying, *"I'll hold you to your promise, otherwise he goes back to Berlin."*

Sarah quietly answered, *"You have my promise and thank you."*

The topic of the young refugee was never discussed until the morning after Simon was deposited on to their doorstep by Rabbi Sackman six weeks later, Sir John was ready to leave for his daily morning walk to his office, Sarah had presented her nephew to his uncle John.

*"That hair must be cut short before anyone sees him, get some English clothes and I've arranged for a private tutor to come to the house to give him English lessons, by the way,"* Sir John continued, *"from now on his name will be Allan Lambert."* *"I've arranged for new documents and identity papers to prove that he's an orphan from my side of the family and we're giving him a home."*

Sir John was giving his wife instructions as if she was one of his minions at the Foreign Office.

*"I want no damned Jews in this house,"* he muttered as he left for his office banging the door behind him, he had not said a single word of greeting to the small boy.

Lady Sarah had not uttered a sound following her husband's tirade, she went over to her young nephew, held him tightly and sobbed her heart out.

"I'll be alright Aunt Sarah," the young boy hadn't understood a word that had been said but tried to assure his aunt in his timid German voice.

She could not answer, how could he know that her tears were not for him, she was venting almost five years of unhappiness and worry for the fate of her family in Berlin.

Sarah eventually stopped sobbing, looked down to the innocent little angel of a boy and realised that her damned husband planned to mould this child into a typical English boy, even to giving him his own surname of Lambert. Her sorrow was tempered by the realisation that the child was at least safe from the Nazis, and as soon as the situation in Germany improved they could both return to Berlin and escape from her husband.

The Rabbi was delighted, the plan had worked to perfection, Sir John had used his position to accept a German Jew with illegal papers and had arranged to provide a false identity, perfect ammunition for blackmailing a senior Foreign Office civil servant who was known to hate all Jews.

For young Simon Schuman, a Jewish refugee from Berlin, his German and Jewish heritage had been eliminated and from now on he would be known as Allan Lambert, an English boy living under the care of his benefactor, the distinguished, Sir John Lambert.

# Chapter Five

# An Exodus From Germany

*"No, No. No!"* Isaac Weisman shouted at his son, Albert, they were sitting in the huge oak panelled study that was the control centre of their jewellery business, Albert had been dreading this conversation with his father, but knew he couldn't put it off any longer, he was thirty years old and the middle child of Isaac and Irene, his sister Sarah was safe in England, she was one year older than him and his younger sister Irene was a widow who refused to leave their father and mother even though she had been persuaded to send her beloved son Simon to sister Sarah in England for safety until one day the persecution of Jews in Germany subsided.

Albert did not agree with his father that the Nazi activities against Jews was only temporary, nor did he have his father's belief that their wealth would shield them for much longer, his father wouldn't face reality. Albert was certain that the latest activities against the Jews of Germany were much more sinister than anything that had gone before, the beatings, vandalism and murders of Jews were escalating every week and Albert had come to a crossroad in his life.

*"Father, I must save my family, I fear so much for our future here in Germany, we can soon return if the situation improves."*

Father and son had been talking for the past two hours, but Albert knew that his father was convinced his loyalty, wealth and standing in the community would save the family from persecution. Albert worshipped his parents and could have changed his plans and relieve his father of heart breaking anguish, but his wife and two children were more important than anything else on earth. Albert was aware that the business would be his when his father retired, after more than a decade of apprenticeship, he knew he could successfully take over, but all their plans and aspirations now had no meaning, he would walk away from affluence and wealth to save his family.

*"Father, I'm definitely taking my family to Palestine while I still can get out of Germany, I'll build a new life in a country that welcomes Jews, it's our promised land. Please! Please! Come with us."*

With tears flowing down his cheeks, Albert hugged his father who had suddenly broken down into a fit of sobbing, his shoulders heaving with emotion, father and son were closer than they had ever been, their grief and heartache created a bond that had been missing, Albert saw this fine upright pillar of strength was suddenly a broken man, a sight he had never seen. He found it strange to be so close and give comfort to his father who had always been in control, rarely showing such deep emotion to his son, the pain was almost too hard to bear.

Isaac had collapsed in his chair, he was suddenly a frail old man, all his resolve had disintegrated, so many friends had emigrated, his grandson was in England and now his beloved son and family planned to leave him and go to Palestine. Isaac was aware that similar situations were being re-enacted by Jews throughout Germany in recent months, now it had invaded his own family and he had to accept the Jews in Germany were in mortal danger and his family were no longer immune.

Albert continued to plead with his father to follow him to Palestine and Isaac reluctantly faced the inevitable. It would soon be 1933, it seemed that Hitler would come to power, he had seen the beatings that the stormtroopers were inflicting on Jews and his moment of decision had arrived, Isaac would soon have his fifty eighth birthday, at that moment he felt twenty years older. The love he felt for his family was unbearable, would he ever see his beloved grandson again, would they ever hug each other and enjoy life as grandparents are meant to do with their grandchildren? If they emigrated, how and where would they live? what about the business? he had a responsibility for his loyal staff? These thoughts and more flooded Isaac's head as he sat in the chair with his dear son's arms holding him tightly. How deeply he loved his son at that moment, the thought of losing him and his beautiful family was unthinkable.

With tears flowing Isaac suddenly rose from his chair, kissed his son on the cheek and without a word opened the safe and took out a box full of jewellery, *"Albert, this is better than money, it will keep you for a long time, go with my love but now, go to your mother and sister."* *"What will you do father?"* With anguish in his voice Albert tried once more to extract a decision from his father, who replied with a weary voice, *"Albert, it's time your mother and I had a long talk, you make your plans, get your family out of Berlin as soon as you can."*

Father and son hugged and cried but could not speak then Albert headed his father to a chair and slowly left the room with words of *"I love you father".*

Within half an hour the study door burst open, *"Now, will you listen to me?"* Isaac's wife was sobbing, Albert had just left the house after breaking the news to his mother and sister. Isaac did not speak, he simply held out his arms to the woman who was his lover, confidante and best friend, they held each other for an age, both were traumatised in their grief and too upset to even speak to each other. Eventually the flood of tears subsided, Irene sat in a chair next to her husband, held his hands and looked at the man she loved dearly, waiting for him to compose himself to reply.

*"Irene, I'm a fool, I should have looked after the family, we could all have been together in a safe country long ago, if only we had gone to America."*

Isaac looked, spoke, and felt so tired, he had been in a long hard fight and lost – Hitler would win.

*"What will you do now, my dear?"* Irene felt so sorry, his patriotism and love of Germany had disintegrated, he looked like a broken man. In quiet tearful voice Isaac replied,

*"I think we should go to England, Sarah can help us settle and her husband's position in the government may help me start a new business."* *"That would be wonderful, and we'll see our dear little Simon again".* Irene was ecstatic, but she refused to travel to England immediately without him, she preferred to wait until Isaac had settled all his business affairs, they would go together or not at all.


Their youngest daughter was delighted at the prospect of seeing her darling Simon again and getting out of Germany but they were all aware that it would take time to settle up the business affairs and arrange to emigrate, but at last the future seemed brighter.

Albert and his family had very little difficulty getting out of Germany and settling in Haifa in Palestine where a group of devout Zionists had established themselves, his wife, Hannah, and the children were happier and more contented than he'd ever seen them. The warm climate and the life style suited them all, but Albert worried for his parents and younger sister, they were still in Berlin, Hitler was now in control and the stories of atrocities against Jews were escalating every day, he'd only be content when he was certain they were safe in England.

# Chapter Six
## Plans Are Halted

Irene Weisman retired to her bed early that night with a feeling of contentment she had not had for a long time, she and Isaac were so happy now that he had decided to go to England. Over the years they had had their highs and lows, but she loved him as dearly as she had done on their wedding day way back in 1901. She had been only twenty one years old and although over thirty years had passed and she had three children, Irene was aware that she'd retained her good looks, complexion and slim figure.

Isaac had been a good husband, loving, caring, but devoted to his business. Over the years he had accumulated a vast wealth and Irene acknowledged that she had enjoyed all the benefits and life style that money allows, but she longed for the day when retirement would bring them even closer and peace in Germany would allow all her dear family to be reunited. As she undressed for bed, Irene felt unwell without identifying the cause but decided it must be the effect of the past twenty four hours. Climbing into bed Irene looked forward to a good night's sleep.

*"Mother is late for breakfast this morning!"* Isaac looked over to his daughter who was busy pouring him a cup of coffee. *"Didn't you wake her when you got up?"* she replied. *"I was very late retiring last night, so I just slept in the guest room rather than disturb her, she needed a good night's sleep."* A few minutes later Isaac said, *"It isn't like her to miss breakfast."* *"Dad, she's just having some extra rest, I'll go up when I finish my coffee."*

Her parents had always been the same, they were more like young lovers, always caring and concerned for each other. Irene longed to see her darling son, but would not dream of leaving her parents alone in Germany, however after last night's decision to emigrate to England she could begin to smile again and look forward to the future.

Finishing her coffee, Irene prepared a breakfast tray, she would give her mother a pleasant surprise this morning, *"I'll take it up to your mother, we need a few moments alone,"* Isaac took the tray, Irene smiled and settled down to enjoy her second cup of coffee.

Isaac slowly climbed the stairs with a feeling of intense love for his wife, she had been a tower of strength for him during their marriage, she had advised, consoled and criticised whenever appropriate, not once had he strayed or even desired to embrace another woman. This morning he intended to tell her how fortunate he was to have such a loyal and tender loving wife.

He opened the door then dropped the tray with such a clatter of breaking crockery that his daughter Irene raced up the stairs and reached her mother almost as quickly as her father. Her feeling of euphoria was gone, she was convinced that her mother was dead, her eyes were closed, mouth open, with blood running from a wound in her forehead, it appeared that she had fallen out of bed.

Isaac seemed to be paralysed by the shock of seeing his wife in such a state, he simply cradled her in his arms and sobbingly repeated her name, over and over again.

Irene quickly established that her mother was still alive, she raced to phone their own doctor because she was well aware that a Jew would get no priority in an emergency hospital.

After what seemed an age, their doctor and a nurse arrived, ushered father and daughter from the bedroom, in total silence Isaac and his daughter sat looking at the bedroom door fearing the worst, the doctor's solemn face produced a sob from Irene, Isaac just stared and waited. Without preamble the doctor gave them the hard facts, he put his hand on Isaac's shoulder and said, *"My friend she has had a severe stroke, I'll need more tests but her speech and movement are greatly affected."* He went on to explain that it would not be wise to send her to hospital, even a place of care was not free of intimidation for a Jew so he advised that she remain in his care at her own home. She would need twenty four hour care and could not be moved for the foreseeable future.

The doctor left the nurse to care for his patient, he would arrange a team of nurses and return within two hours with a specialist for more tests.

Father and daughter stood looking down at Irene without speaking, tears flowing down their cheeks without a sound from either of them, in twenty four hours their world had collapsed, euphoria had been replaced by despair, the happiness of the previous night was now a misery too hard to bear.

The specialist confirmed that Irene's disability was of major proportions, she had no speech or movement down the left side of her body and she was in a state of total confusion.

*"I'm afraid that's out of the question"* was the unequivocal reply to Isaac's disclosure of their plans to emigrate to England, nor could the specialist give an estimate on how long it would be before she could be moved without the risk of another possible fatal stroke.

The nursing and medical care was as good as money could buy. Condolences, cards and flowers were received on a daily basis from friends, acquaintances and business contacts, but daughter Irene was well aware of the real tragedy. She and her father had not spoken about the one thought dominating both minds, if her mother could not be moved with safety, what about their plans to go to England?

What should she do, stay with her father and mother or join her dear son Simon and her sister Sarah, time was running short if she intended to abandon her father and mother, a decision was required without delay.

The speed of change in Germany took the decision away from Irene, Hitler's elevation to power resulted in an escalation of anti-Jewish laws and legislation, even the attitude of ordinary German people suddenly placed every Jew in mortal danger.

# *Chapter Seven*
## *"You Can't Do That"*

The Hitler regime targeted the Jews immediately they took control of the country in January 1933 and because of his wealth Isaac was one of the first to feel the impact, he was required to list all his assets on threat of imprisonment if anything was omitted. He knew his bank account, stocks and shares could be checked, his shops were public knowledge but the jewellery in his safe was known to him and no one else so he persuaded his daughter to sew jewels into their clothing with the hope that the Nazis would never know.

His daughter had resigned herself to the fact that she couldn't abandon her father and mother, her letter to sister Sarah in England had given details of their situation and pleaded that she take care of her son until she could move their mother and leave Germany.

Sarah replied with assurances but did not want to add to their burden by disclosing that her husband hated Jews, that Simon was now known as Allan Lambert and was being educated as an English boy.

Over the next few years the German people were euphoric, Hitler promised power, wealth and employment for everyone, he built up the armed forces and took control of every aspect of daily life, he put Germany on a roller coaster to success and the vast majority of Germans were delighted.

As part of their deliberate strategy the Nazis blamed the Jews not only for the problems in Germany but problems world wide. A Jew was portrayed as lower than a rat in the sewer and the propaganda was so effective the German people believed and began to hate and treat Jews accordingly.

One of the specialists treating Irene suddenly disappeared never to be seen again, only those nurses who were Jews continued on the daily rota of care and even they demanded payment on a daily basis. As month followed month Irene showed little sign of improvement, she could not feed herself, although with help she could use a wheel chair to be pushed into the garden. She spoke with her eyes and indicated constant anguish, her love for Isaac and her daughter was obvious, but all they could do was to hold her hand, with repeated words of comfort and reassurance that she would be alright.

Communication with Sarah in England and Albert in Palestine was now impossible, all mail in or out of the country for Jews was intercepted or simply confiscated, the Gestapo was slowly isolating all Jews in Germany.

*"You can't do that, I have a legal right to every shop in my business!"*

Isaac had been summoned to the Central Office of Administration to be informed that the state was taking over his business, because of the size of his empire he was one of the first to be notified that a decree was being issued the next day banning all Jews from owning a business.

*"I'm a loyal German, you can't do this!"* Isaac shouted with all the emotion he could muster, the man behind the counter nodded to a man sitting at the end of the office, the half dozen German people in the large office fell silent. The stocky man dressed in a long, black leather coat and a black leather trilby hat walked up behind Isaac and quietly whispered, *"follow me to sort out your problem or I'll shoot you here."*

Isaac was so startled, he was on his way to a side door before he realised, the door led to some stairs down to a boiler room, as soon as the door closed the Gestapo man gave a hard push that sent Isaac head over heels hitting every stair on the way down. At the bottom of the stairs the man hardly raised his voice, simply hissed into Isaac's ear over and over again, *"You're not a German, you're a Jew", "You're not a German, you're a Jew".* With every word Isaac was kicked in the head and every inch of his body until he sank in merciful oblivion.

The battered body of Isaac was found in a nearby side street with a piece of cardboard tied around his neck with the words 'I am a Jew' written in red paint.

Irene was hysterical when two friends delivered Isaac in a wheelbarrow to his home. Although still alive he was in a dreadful state, no hospital would take him and only their daily nurses could give him care. She did not dare tell her mother for fear of another stroke and was in a dilemma, she had never been involved in the business and had no knowledge of their finances. She contacted the senior manager in their largest store in Berlin and asked for his help.

Fritz Hyde arrived the next morning precisely at 9.am as arranged. Irene stared in disbelief, he was dressed in the uniform of a Gestapo officer, with a swastika armband and revolver in a holster, four armed soldiers were behind him. She could not speak and waited for him to explain, she did not really know the man except that her father held him in high regard having employed him from being a boy apprentice who had been so efficient and enthusiastic that he had reached the highest management position in the company.

His tone of voice belied his image, his closeness to her father over so many years seemed to be a slight embarrassment, but his message was stark, brutal and not for discussion.

*"Fraulein Weisman, you are required to vacate this property within seven days, you no longer own a business, your bank account is closed and all your assets are confiscated, you are allowed only one suitcase each*

*and you will be notified tomorrow of the address of the apartment allocated to you."*

He returned to his Nazi image by almost yelling *"Heil Hitler"* gave the Nazi salute, turned on his heel and accompanied by his bodyguard climbed into their vehicle and drove off.

Irene sank slowly to the floor at the open door, she sobbed uncontrollably, only the arrival of her mother's nurse almost an hour later brought the distraught woman back to reality. She was in total confusion, at a loss to understand, comprehend or act on the information she had been given from the man who owed his whole working success to her father. She did not need to contact friends because they began to contact her father in the expectation of soliciting his help.

Every Jewish family in the neighbourhood had been visited by the Gestapo with the same ultimatum, all of their assets had been confiscated, they must vacate their property and move to an area in East Berlin. They would all be controlled in a designated ghetto, in addition it had been decreed that all Jews would wear a yellow 'Star of David' on their clothing, and many other orders were issued, all designed to humiliate and isolate the whole Jewish population of Germany.

The result was fear and panic, some very old and unstable people committed suicide by jumping out of windows, others simply walked from their homes never to be seen again. All Jews were dismissed from universities, all retail businesses were liquidated and Jewish children were expelled from state schools. Any Jew who had a doubt about the intentions of the Nazis could no longer ignore what was happening, this was ethnic cleansing on a ruthless and systematic scale of historic proportions. Zionists called on all Jews to go to Palestine and for those who had moved before the Nazi clamp down this was a lifesaver and as Jews flooded into 'their promised land'. Little was it realised that this mass influx of Jews into Palestine would produce more ethnic cleansing in the future except it would be perpetrated by the Jews against the Palestinians.

Irene was in turmoil, her mother was an invalid needing constant care and attention, her father was so battered and bruised he could hardly move, they were being forced to get out of their beautiful home and she had little or no money, their business and fortune had been seized and she had to vacate within days. Their servants had already returned to help their own families and the nurses ceased their caring at the first sign of a Gestapo officer, the Weisman family had hit rock bottom or so Irene thought.

Similar to hundreds of Jewish families, Irene tried to sell anything and everything she could, some of their beautiful furniture, carpets and paintings were bought by German people for a pittance, she was more fortunate than some families who were beaten up and all their belongings stolen from them.

Irene selected the three largest suitcases in the house, and put a few clothes, with jewels sewn into the linings into each case, on the theory that if one case was stolen or lost she would still have some jewels to sell, she then carefully selected the items she and her father and mother would consider essential to survival. Her main concern was for her parents, she didn't think her mother could comprehend what was happening but the shock of moving into new surroundings could prove fatal, her father was barely alive after his savage beating, she tried to speak to him but it was to no avail. She spent that night sitting on a chair with her mother in bed at one side and her father on a couch at her other side, frightened and fearful for their future, all her thoughts were on her beloved son, growing up in England away from her but at least he was safe from whatever lay in front of them here in Nazi Germany.

At six o'clock the next morning a loud banging on the door

_My Son The Enemy_

produced a Gestapo officer with a lorry already half full of Jews, Irene was instructed to climb onto the back of the lorry with her father, mother and three suitcases. Her protests that the cases were too heavy and that her mother and father couldn't get on the high lorry resulted in Irene being punched on the face, dislodging two front teeth and a loud order to four soldiers who literally picked up Irene's parents and the three suitcases and flung them among the dozen wailing and crying Jews already there.

Even as this happened, a high ranking officer was inspecting the Weisman mansion in preparation for his own occupancy, he had already placed a guard to ensure that German looters did not ransack the beautiful residence.

Irene was fearful for her father and mother; the other Jewish occupants on the lorry were too engrossed in their own problems and future to help or show concern for others; men, women and half a dozen children were crying, praying, or silently staring into space. Irene tried to comfort her parents who were lying on the floor of the lorry and feeling every bump and pothole of the journey, she barely had the desire to stop the blood flowing from her mouth which was already swelling up and painful.

After a seemingly endless journey the lorry came to a shuddering halt and stopped amidst utter chaos, screaming, yelling soldiers and barking dogs. At least twenty other lorries had hundreds of Jews disembarking and being forced to line up to be told their accommodation, Irene was desperate to see to her parents who could hardly move, she was equally concerned for their suitcases, without them they were penniless.

Eventually with pushing and prodding by soldiers the Weisman family, together with their precious suitcases were deposited into their future place of residence, one bedroom and a kitchen, a far cry from the luxury of their mansion, servants and wealth.

All that Irene could wonder was *"Why us, we're Germans and human beings, what have we done wrong other than being born Jewish?"*

# Chapter Eight
# Converted To An Englishman

Sarah was desperate for news of her family in Germany. Newspaper stories in England painted unbelievable horror pictures of the Jews by the Nazis. She had kept her promise to her husband John, and accompanied him at state functions and organised dinner parties when required, but her hate for him had not diminished, she still refused to share his bed and could not bear him to show any affection. Her pleading for him to obtain information from Berlin about her family fell on his deaf ears, even though his authority in the foreign office could have made contact, his loathing for Jews was still intense, he had no intention of using his position to satisfy her.

She had some consolation however that at least her nephew was safe, but she only saw him on school holidays, her damned husband had changed the boy's image, life-style and even his name, she longed to tell the boy the truth but was terrified her husband would carry out his threat and send him back to Berlin. One day she vowed that Simon (she could never accept his new name of Allan) would be told the whole truth about his nationality, religion and name.

Allan Lambert would soon be thirteen years old and almost eight years had passed since he had travelled from Berlin to England, memories of his early young life were fading, he remembered a big mansion but images of his mother and grandparents were now distorted. The constant training on speech, image and attitude had eliminated his knowledge of the German language, his Jewish faith and background, he was a typical English boy with an apparent distinguished uncle as his guardian at an impressive private school in Surrey.

He spoke impeccable English, dressed as befitting his background and was a very popular young man, academically above the norm, keen on sport with a confidence that good education and affluence provide, but he was aware of the one thing for which he craved – love.

His life was at boarding school only seeing his Aunt Sarah on holidays, and although she showed him some affection there always seemed an invisible barrier, he stopped asking about his family because she refused any discussion as if she was fearful about something. Life was good with his friends at boarding school, he was with a group of six boys, all with similar interests but with different backgrounds, a banker, factory owner, even the son of a lord, all parents who were affluent and providing the best education for their sons. Away from their studies, conversation was centred around girls, cricket and more and more arguments about Germany and the prospects of war, some boys, including Allan, couldn't wait to reach the age of seventeen and join the army as young soldiers.

Allan was convinced that a career as an army officer would be ideal, particularly now that war with Germany seemed inevitable.

More and more, the older boys were taking sides for and against the few Jewish students. Influenced by newspaper stories some taunted the Jewish boys, blaming their race for the world's troubles and forcing tutors to warn against intimidation, but although Allan had some sympathy for the Jewish students he had no firm opinion either way, but was well aware that a hatred of Jews ran very deep with some boys, maybe fuelled by their parents. The press reports about the Nazi treatment of Jews in Germany were always offset by the overwhelming opinion that *"it couldn't possibly be as bad as newspaper stories made out, because they always exaggerated."*

His Uncle John's arranged tuition had been so successful that Allan had no doubt that he was English and an orphan but longed to know more about his parents, his Aunt Sarah occasionally dropped hints about an uncle living abroad but immediately he asked questions she closed the discussion, Allan had made his mind up however, once he had reached the age of 21 years he would make his own enquiries.

On September 3rd 1939 Britain declared war on Germany, Allan was fourteen years old and his boarding school was considered to be a safe location with the result that he saw less of his Aunt Sarah and Uncle John. He simply got on with his studies with his declared aim to join the army and become an officer before the war ended.

The early stages of the war had little effect on Allan, rationing simply encouraged the school cook to be more adventurous, they had regular air raid rehearsals that resulted in everyone sitting in a cold and dingy cellar wearing gas masks for half an hour then emerge into fresh air having completed their war exercise for the week. Most boys were interested in the progress of the war, in fact two tutors really entered into war euphoria by allocating an area called the 'War Room' where maps, charts and updated bulletins were displayed and used in discussion groups. It was generally agreed that the war would not last more than a year (much to Allan's dismay), after all Britain had beaten Germany in World War One and there was no way they could withstand the might of the British Empire a second time. The only tangible effect on Allan was to see more and more people in uniform when he visited the local town or on his visits to Aunt Sarah in London. Three tutors disappeared into the armed forces to be replaced by retired tutors who showed wild enthusiasm at their new lease of life. Gossip swept around the school when a prominent Jewish boy departed in floods of tears, his 'best' friend wasted no time informing the 'War Room' group that the boy's father had been interned by the government for 'security reasons'. He, along with dozens of immigrants from Germany were interrogated to establish their links or sympathy with Nazi Germany, some were released, but many were not given freedom until the end of the war.

For the next three years Allan had to curb his enthusiasm to join the army. Studies, exams and the progress of the war filled his young life, every high and low point of the fighting was analysed in minute detail by the students who attended the school 'War Room'. Hitler's success in Europe, the fall of France, Denmark, General Montgomery's success at El-Alamein and the back-to-the-wall Battle of Britain had every student feeling they were involved without leaving the calm serenity of scholastic life. The occasional trauma of a boy called to the headmaster's study to receive the sad news that a father or relative had been killed made everyone aware that war wasn't a 'War Room' game. The day news arrived that a tutor had been killed in an air battle brought the school to a standstill, lessons were cancelled and a church parade with a long sermon on the horrors of war brought total gloom over the whole school.

The rare visits to see Aunt Sarah in London gave Allan his real experience of the effects of war on the civilian population, he saw his uncle John only occasionally, the foreign office was now almost his permanent home, when they did meet their conversation was in monosyllables, Allan could never understand his uncle's antagonism towards him. The joy on Aunt Sarah's face every time Allan arrived made it a worthwhile journey, rationing appeared to be non-existent in her kitchen, Allan learned that in spite of the war, she still provided a degree of socialising for her husband's friends and colleagues and a special food allowance was provided for ministers and senior civil servants. The constant sound of sirens warning of an air raid resulted in the whole household descending to a shelter that had been specially reinforced for senior government personnel and their families. It was in stark contrast to the air raid shelter at Allan's school, carpeted floor, comfortable chairs, reading material, heating, lighting and even food, in case their stay would be a lengthy one. However the luxury trappings did not eliminate the terror Allan experienced every time he heard the crunch of an exploding bomb above his head and the sight of devastated buildings all over London made him realise his good fortune at being away in quiet Surrey. When leaving his Aunt Sarah he always pleaded with her to leave London, but she claimed that her duty was at the side of her husband. Allan would never know that he was only safe because of the deal she had made with her husband to get Allan out of Germany in 1930, she did not dare break her promise even though her life was miserable and she was in constant state of terror.

In 1942 Allan celebrated his seventeenth birthday with a small party of his close friends at school. He received a card with some money from Aunt Sarah and could not wait to join the army and train to be an officer.

An invasion of Europe was considered imminent, and Allan desperately wanted to become involved before the war ended. He passed the medical examination, made his goodbyes to everyone at school and reported to Budbrooke Barracks in Warwick, little did he know that his army career would be totally different to his expectation, his past life would catch up to him in the most dramatic way and he would face an awesome decision.

# My Son The Enemy

David Hughes

# Chapter Nine
## Death In The Ghetto

During the growing up of Allan Lambert, the progress of the war and world wide press and radio coverage, the one item of glaring omission was the lack of news of the treatment of Jews in Germany, the few details that occasionally emerged were so horrendous they were dismissed as media exaggeration. Sarah received terrible stories from her Rabbi friend but news of her family in Berlin was impossible to obtain, she was afraid for her own life in London because of the German bombers and fearful for her family in Germany from the thousands of bombs being dropped on Berlin by the British Air Force. Her husband dismissed her fears by saying it was out of his hands, what he did not say was that British intelligence was confirming the stories leaking from Germany about "the Jewish problem".

Allan Lambert was unaware of the fact that he was a German Jew by birth with his mother and grandparents at the other side of a war zone, a war he could not wait to join. In addition his uncle and family were in Palestine and actively involved with a terrorist organisation fighting the British army.

"The Jewish Problem" existed in Germany from the day Hitler had entered politics but escalated when he took control of Germany. The German publics endorsement of Hitler's anti-Jewish policy was in November 1938, the so- called "Kristallnacht Riots" (night of broken glass) when Jews were attacked indiscriminately throughout Germany, more than a thousand synagogues were burned and ransacked,

45

7500 shops had windows broken, stock looted, never to re-open and hundreds of Jewish men, women and children were battered, bruised and killed, there was no doubt that the Nazis had a sinister agenda aimed at every German Jew. Allan's mother, Irene with her mother and father were some of the early victims of the Nazis, her father had his jewellery business confiscated, their mansion taken over and the family had gone from a state of incredible wealth to abject poverty, housed in a one bedroom apartment within a Jewish ghetto controlled by the Nazis. Irene's father was slowly recovering from his attack by a Gestapo officer, but he was a broken man, never leaving the apartment and depending completely on his beloved daughter for everything, her mother was totally incapacitated, she had never recovered from her massive stroke and seemed to have little understanding of their situation. Irene was their nurse, cook and carer with a constant fear for their lives and a daily thought for her son in England well aware he was growing up. She wondered what he now looked like, did he remember her, would she ever see him again?

Their life in the ghetto was a daily struggle for survival and a constant battle against fear, the ghetto was completely sealed from the outside world, with every exit either bricked up or guarded by members of the S.S. Only a select band of Jews were allowed a daily permit to leave the ghetto if they were doing work for special German families or business with the inevitability that they were used to barter and handle contraband for those Jews who still possessed something of value.

Irene had succeeded in keeping secret the jewels stitched into her clothing at the behest of her father many months ago and shrewdly disposed of them one at a time and always through a different courier, she only received a fraction of the true value of each piece of jewellery but the result was the difference between starvation or survival. In the ghetto there was no means of working for a living, they were not issued with a ration card for meat and the bread, sugar and other food allowances were less than half that allowed to German citizens, the Jews were being slowly starved to death, and at least fifty a day died from malnutrition alone. The overall conditions were appalling, with very little clean drinking water, overcrowding and a scarcity of fuel and medicines, disease was rife and the overall daily death rate very high.

Some form of control and discipline was created by ghetto Jewish leaders and a Jewish police force but as these were all selected and appointed by the Nazis with whom they were forced to co-operate, the fine line between co-operation and collaboration was constantly being questioned.

Fear of the Nazis was a way of life for the Jews, face slapping, ridicule and clubbing with a rifle butt was a routine daily torture. The real fear was when trucks were moved into the ghetto and S.S. guards with fierce snarling dogs, indiscriminately rounded up men, women and children, forced them onto the trucks and drove out, leaving mothers crying out for children and families sobbing for loved ones departed. They were never seen again and one story that had percolated the ghetto by a courier was now accepted as fact, apparently the unfortunate Jews who had been taken, were transported to a forest where a ditch had been dug, they were made to strip and in groups of four, were marched to the edge of the ditch and shot. Hundreds were disposed of in this manner, consequently whenever the trucks arrived everyone scattered for their lives.

For Irene, her mother and father, life was marginally better than the vast majority of ghetto inmates, the slow disposal of jewels ensured that they were not at starvation level, but she had to be ultra careful to avoid the suspicion of Germans who would put them on to the next truck if discovered, and if Jews who were starving found out, she would be lynched. There was fighting in the ghetto over a mouldy loaf of bread, so Irene's hoard of jewellery would have sparked a riot. Irene's mother was so frail she could not stand and spent most of the day in bed and would not have eaten if Irene had not spoon-fed her some watery soup. "Soup again?" Isaac constantly complained to his daughter without realising their predicament, he had lost all sense of reality, never leaving their apartment and spending his days recalling the past to anyone who would listen. Irene was very close to breaking point, she made certain her parents were fed every day, but she was beginning to look like a skeleton and malnutrition was taking its toll. She was terrified that one day the Nazis would enter their apartment and that would be the end, any hope she had of seeing her son would be lost, he would now be sixteen years old and the ache in her heart to see him was worse than her fear of the Nazis even the British bombs had less fear for her, many times she hoped a bomb could put them all out of their misery.

Every day was a repetition of the previous one, the misery, fear and hopelessness was on the face of everyone, laughter and happiness was a luxury long forgotten, their only activity and thoughts were for friends and loved ones exterminated by the Nazis, how to survive for the next twenty four hours and the constant battle to rid the body of lice. Irene was well aware neither she nor her mother and father could endure their existence for much longer, it was a miracle that her mother was still alive with such limited medication and lack of food, thankfully she wasn't suffering mentally because she was in a world of her own. Her father was frail and she could see his mental capacity was deteriorating every day, as for herself, Irene knew that her body could not take much more, the physical burden of caring for her parents, lack of food, the mental torture, fear of the Nazis and the constant thoughts of her son was taking its toll. If the Nazis planned to exterminate all Jews, then in her low moments of depression Irene prayed *"Please God, let it be now."*

The Nazis' policy aimed at eliminating Jews was planned down to the last detail, one of the first concentration camps was Dachau opened in March 1933 and housed enemies of the Nazis, mainly communists. One year later Heinrich Himmler created an *'inspectorate of concentration camps'* with a plan to create a central command of all camps and provide special training for the guards. The next phase, one year later was the creation of the *'Nuremberg Laws'* which defined who was considered to be a Jew, at the same time it cancelled the few citizens' rights they still possessed. Julius Streigher planned and controlled all anti-Jewish and racial propaganda encouraging the ordinary German citizens to hate the Jews. In 1939 a statement by the German foreign ministry declared *"The ultimate aim of its German Jewish policy was the emigration of all Jews in Germany"*. Himmler was put in charge of the planned mass killing, at the same time seven camps were built including Buchenwald.

The fate of Irene, her father, mother and millions of Jews had been decided.

October 1942 was the month that Allan Lambert entered Budbrook Barracks in Warwick on his first step towards becoming an officer in the British army. In the same month and the same year his mother Irene, and his grandparents in Berlin were about to face disaster.

Unknown to Irene the latest courier to whom she had entrusted a jewel to exchange for food had been discovered and shot but not before being tortured to disclose the source of the precious stone.

Screeching tyres, snarling dogs and the loud clatter of jackboots on the stairs was the preview to the apartment door being burst open with a rifle butt followed by a short period of eerie silence that to Irene seemed to be an eternity as she cowered in the corner of their room.

An immaculately dressed high ranking S.S. officer strolled into the apartment as if he was on a social visit, he stood in the centre of the room surveying the scene of poverty, looked at Irene's father sitting in a chair with his head bowed, turning to see Irene's mother lying on the bed giving him a vacant stare, then he looked at Irene standing in the corner of the room, her body visibly shaking from top to toe, her eyes staring in absolute fear. He withdrew the gun from his holster, slowly walked over to Irene's mother, pointed it to her temple and said to Irene, *"You have three minutes to give me any jewels in your possession."* Irene almost dove into the cupboard in her desperation and seemed to take an age to identify the correct clothing and place it at his feet. *"They are all in the lining sir,"* she said in a voice almost too quiet to hear. His ice cold stare was everlasting and the quietness of his reply was more intimidating than if he had been shouting and surrounded by fierce dogs.

*"You have broken the law and will be punished"* he said, as if he was reprimanding a child, *"Be ready to move at daybreak tomorrow."*

*"Please sir, my mother cannot be moved"* Irene pleaded with tears flowing down her face.

Without a word the S.S. officer walked over to Irene's mother, shot her dead and walked from the apartment without a comment or backward glance, two soldiers picked up the clothing and the fading clatter of their jackboots produced a silence so intense it could be touched.

The small room had the choking smell from gunfire, Irene had collapsed onto the floor, her eyes bulging at the sight of her mother, whose face had been blown away.

Irene was too traumatised to grieve or have any other human emotion, she was in a complete trance when next morning Nazi soldiers threw her father and her on to the back of a lorry with their only possessions being the clothes they were wearing, they felt they had reached rock bottom.

# Chapter Ten
# Transport To Concentration Camp

Irene lay on the floor of the lorry for what seemed a life time, there were no stops for food, drink or toilet, but she was beyond the needs of a human being, death at that moment would have been bliss and an end to her torment. The image of her murdered mother dominated her mind, the shock and heartache at such a violent and sudden departure of the woman she loved more than life itself had Irene only a hairsbreadth from insanity.

The shuddering, braking of the lorry brought her back from the brink and the realisation that she was not alone in her misery. The German guards dropped the tailgate of the lorry. With shouting, prodding with rifles and kicking they forced Irene, her father and the other miserable souls to become participants in a scene from hell.

They were on a railway siding, a train of cattle wagons with doors wide open were awaiting their occupation, German soldiers with fixed bayonets lined the platform while others herded hundreds of Jewish men, women and children on to the train. The mixture of sounds created a picture of unimaginable horror, with screams of frightened people, crying children, snarling dogs and yelling soldiers cracking whips on the backs of anyone not running fast enough from lorry to train. Overseeing the whole operation was an immaculately uniformed senior S.S. officer, a huge snarling dog at his side, a cigar in his mouth and a revolver in his hand, he was obviously satisfied with the efficiency of his organisation.

Irene held on tight to her father's hand, terrified they may be separated, he stumbled a couple of times and she screamed in terror when a slavering dog was within inches of mauling Isaac. There were so many frightened people running, they were falling and bumping into each other, one woman near Irene was holding a little boy with one hand, a baby in the other, and was exhausted. Irene offered to carry the baby but with wild eyes the mother refused to hand over the child in case they became separated.

Occasionally a sudden silence descended when the loud crack of a gun-shot overshadowed every other noise, the adrenalin rush of soldiers caught up in the melee took them far beyond the bounds of humanity, and the disabled, slow movers and even abandoned children were despatched with a single bullet, nothing was allowed to delay the train's departure.

With a feeling of absolute exhaustion, Irene was bundled on to one of the cattle wagons behind her father, at least they were together and whatever their destination, surely life could not get worse. The floor was covered by a thick layer of straw, the only toilet facility was a huge pail that emitted a shocking smell of disinfectant and the crush of people in each wagon made it impossible to sit down. Suddenly the door was closed with an almighty bang followed by the clang of locks being applied and within minutes the train was moving, they were in complete darkness, terrified and unaware of their destination.

The train shuddered to a halt as daybreak emerged, doors were flung open for the Jewish passengers to be herded on to a platform by German soldiers with the inevitable shouting and snarling dogs. Their morning torment was almost a relief after the horror of the night time train journey, embarrassment had soon disappeared as the call of nature demanded the need to use the toilet facility and within a short time the smell of disinfectant was overwhelmed by a stench so overpowering it caused vomiting on to the straw covered floor. Sleep had been impossible, Irene was now in a state of semi-consciousness, it seemed impossible for her to accept reality. Throughout the night she had stood, eyes closed, holding her father's hand and swaying with the weight of humanity packed so tightly they were almost as one, in the dim distance of her mind she was aware of the sounds of distress, children crying, adults moaning, praying and the occasional scream of a tormented soul in utter despair. Within one hour Irene and her father were back on the train, Isaac had not uttered a word, held his daughter's hand and did her bidding as they lined up for water, a chunk of stale bread and a bowl of weak soup, he seemed to be in a world of his own.

Irene became oblivious to the passing of time, days and nights merged into a morass of screams, moans and total despair, personal hygiene and dignity were abandoned as was life itself, every few hours a low distinctive moan signalled the end of another poor soul who could take no more. Every morning the disposal of the dead created more space for the living, lack of food and water seemed to be a secondary problem compared to the overwhelming fear as to their fate awaiting at journey's end. Irene was convinced that her father was near the end of his tether, he held her hand so tightly it hurt, didn't utter a word and looked so sad and forlorn. She had no tears left to shed, but every inch of her body ached with sadness, she hated the Nazis with a passion, yet was pleased that her dear mother had died so quickly and been saved from this torture, but to see her father who had been such a pillar of strength, dignity and wisdom, now reduced to a pathetic skeleton was heartbreaking. She was convinced she would never see her beloved son Simon again, in fact she deliberately avoided including him in her thoughts and prayers, even the act of remembering was too painful.

Journey's end was at Mauthausen concentration camp, and was used to provide slave labour for local industry, however there was no work for old, young or infirm Jews, for them this was the end of the line. To provide an air of calm, a band was playing soothing music, shouting soldiers and snarling dogs were noticeable by their absence, in their place were emaciated Jewish men in striped pyjama-like clothes who helped them off the wagons and directed them to a place to stand in line, armed S.S. soldiers quietly oversaw the whole operation. *"Say you have a trade!"* an almost inaudible whisper was passed on to Irene from an old man who directed her to a line of women and gently eased her father's hand from his tight grip on her. *"He can get a ride on the lorry, he seems to be too exhausted to walk."*

The man's face was gentle, full of compassion with tear filled dark eyes, Irene didn't question his instruction she was overwhelmed at this sudden act of caring in a world she thought had abandoned human kindness. Standing with a group of terrified women she suddenly realised that the queue of lorries were taking old men, women, disabled people and very young children, mothers were hysterical being parted from loved ones, Irene panicked and moved to retrieve her father. She had only made two steps when one of the overseeing S.S. officers blocked her path and in a quiet but brutal voice said, *"take one more step and I'll shoot you."*

At that moment, all the stories and rumours of Nazi death camps became a reality, it could not happen to her family, the rumours were exaggerated, no human being could be so crude as the stories had suggested. Irene turned icy cold, choking with a dread she had never experienced, with the realisation the stories were true, the Nazis were exterminating the Jews and she was living the nightmare.

She tried in vain to see her dear father but the lorries moved off down a tree lined avenue towards some long buildings with two high chimneys, leaving long lines of men and women, some like Irene, standing in a trance, others quietly sobbing and many with eyes closed making a contact with their God. Immediately the lorries disappeared, the music stopped and the S.S. officers took control, slowly walking down the line, they made three selections that determined, immediate death, being worked to death or some hope of survival.

Anyone who appeared to be weak or unstable was directed to more waiting lorries, those with a trade were instructed to stay where they were and the rest were marched off to some barracks at the edge of the camp. Irene claimed she was a daughter of a jeweller and had a full knowledge of jewellery, this saved her from being marched away for slave labour where life expectancy was no more than six months.

The reception area was a sham, designed to create calm, the music, green grass, trees, lack of shouting and barking dogs ensured that the lorries drove off with passengers reassured they'd be alright, others marched off, unaware they were heading for slave labour.

Although the train had transported thousands of Jews of all ages, Irene was left standing with thirty men and women who had claimed to have a trade (tailors, shoemakers, seamstresses, etc.). Her heart was pounding with the fear that she would be found out, her knowledge of jewellery was no more than any woman, but if God was on her side she would survive for a few more days.

The S.S. officers and guarding soldiers marched away leaving the 'Kapo' to take over. Among the inmates of the camp were politicians, criminals and homosexuals, from whom the Nazis selected 'Kapo Guards' who were feared as much as the S.S. With heavy clubs and a brutality created from their own fear of death if they failed in their duty, it was ironic that these Jewish inmates inflicted incredible acts of brutality, fear and occasional death to fellow Jewish men and women. A female 'Kapo' guard marched the women behind the reception area to a scene of pure horror that convinced Irene she'd never leave the camp alive.

The smell of death was overwhelming, the sight of walking skeletons in striped pyjamas unbelievable and the blanket of collective misery was stifling. Irene was taken to a hut where three women and one man were sorting through a huge pile of jewellery. *"Put her to work until I come back"* the 'Kapo' guard barked to the male inmate, and marched out to the shoe block next door. David was thirty years old and looked twice his age, after two years in the camp he had a permanent stoop due to constantly looking down at the ground and spoke in an almost inaudible whisper. Irene looked positively healthy compared to her fellow workers and it did not take long for them to realise her knowledge of jewellery was non-existent compared to their life-long experience in the business. To her relief they agreed to show her how to sort costume from the real jewellery and David did the final specialist selection for the benefit of the camp Commander. They were not allowed to communicate but with one woman on the look out Irene whispered as much information as she could concerning the situation outside and they gave her a graphic description of camp life.

Inmates of the camp slept in long huts with wooden bunks, the floor and beds were covered with straw and only one blanket per person was issued for all weathers. Some huts were so overcrowded that two and three people slept on one bunk making it impossible to turn throughout the night, men and women were forced to sleep in the same hut. There were two roll calls outside every day and no matter how bad the weather they were forced to stand in line until the guards were satisfied that everyone had been accounted for. Everyone in the camp was classified by the colour of a star sewn on to their camp uniform of striped pyjamas;

**Politicians - Red : Criminals - Green :**

**Homosexuals - Pink : Jews - Yellow.**

Leaders from political prisoners were selected by the Nazis to be responsible for keeping order in each block, the whole camp was surrounded by an electrified fence that was the final destination of those who could take no more. The belongings of everyone were taken when they entered the camp and the lucky 'skilled' ones were employed on sorting everything out to be re-used by German civilians.

With sadness, David explained to Irene the true purpose of the camp and the final destination of the Jews who had been driven away on the lorries. They had been off loaded outside the long brick building and told that to avoid typhus, everyone must strip naked and enter the showers. With utter embarrassment and fear the doors were locked after entering the shower, inmates were gassed and incinerated. To emphasise the story, David took Irene to a window to see smoke belching from the tall chimneys, upon which she collapsed sobbing to the floor, realising she would never see her beloved father again.

*"You come with me".* The Kapo guard returned and pushed Irene out of the door to a small hut where she was stripped naked by a male 'Kapo' guard who leeringly issued her with a dirty striped dress with a yellow star stitched on, he then grabbed her arm and tattooed a number on her forearm. She was no longer a person with a name, she was concentration camp prisoner No. 17235892 whose life belonged to her Nazi guards.

# My Son The Enemy

# Chapter Eleven
# The Jewish Problem

In 1942, Sir John Lambert was sixty one years old and planned to retire in four years time, provided the war was ended with victory for the Allies, he was already cultivating the right connections in order to be elevated to the House of Lords, as a fitting reward for his dedication to the civil service. His career had gone according to plan, from the day he rang the bell at the orphanage, following the death of his parents to now, he had planned every step meticulously and was proud of the fact he had been so successful, but on the way his path was littered with people wronged and enemies created.

Not least was Sarah who he had married for sheer convenience, he had no regrets or remorse, the marriage had served his purpose, she had got a title, a good living and had been saved from the Nazis. He was unaware of her return to the Jewish faith and would have been devastated had he known of the confidentialities she had divulged to her Rabbi friend, who in turn relayed everything to a terrorist group in Palestine.

Even the naturalisation and documentation of Sarah's nephew was beyond question, he was confident that his identity, would never be associated with a Jewish father.

His hatred for the Jews was as intense as it had been from the days when they had taunted him in the slums of the East-end of London when he was a young boy. As an adviser in the Foreign Office, only his brilliance in organisation and international knowledge outweighed his anti-Semitic views which were well known throughout government circles. However, he was not alone, many high ranking members of parliament and the civil service were quietly anti-Semitic and would not lift a finger to help the Jews, but Sir John and a few other influential people openly voiced their Jewish opinions and were prepared to take action to further their hatred.

As far back as the 1930s the British government were well aware of the situation in Germany, and although concern was expressed, some people in power were anti-Semitic and urged the Turks to turn back to sea a Jewish refugee ship which sank in the Black Sea with the loss of 767 Jews. A few years later a plan to 'buy' the freedom of an Hungarian Jewish Community from the Gestapo was ignored. Although a government memo in 1938 (one year before the outbreak of war) says –

*"The question of illegal Jewish immigration is becoming a serious problem, conditions in Germany are stimulating large numbers of Jews to emigrate as emigrants."*

At the same time British officials in Palestine turned away thousands of Jews fleeing the Nazis, and even sent gunships to set them adrift on the high seas.

In 1939 when war was declared, borders were sealed, trapping Sarah's family and thousands of Jews, Sir John was aware of the atrocities, chose to do nothing to help his wife's parents and sister. He felt he had done enough for her family by saving her and the Jewish brat.

However, not all members of the government closed their eyes to the atrocities, more and more stories were filtering through to convince a delegation to demand a serious investigation into all known facts and intelligence information. A full picture eventually emerged of the size, scale and horror of the holocaust but even then it was decided that the only way to save the Jews of occupied Europe was to end the war as quickly as possible, the inmates of the concentration camps would have to wait.

It was clearly realised that come the end of the war with anticipated victory, a major problem would arise, how to disperse and control the thousand of Jewish survivors from the concentration camps? Many of whom would wish to settle in their 'promised land' of Palestine.

Who better to head the committee charged with finding a solution to the 'Jewish problem' than the experienced, distinguished Sir John Lambert.

Sir John was delighted, he considered the task to be the successful culmination of his career.

# Chapter Twelve

# Army Training

*"Do you mind if I take this bed?"* Allan Lambert queried, *"No problem"* Harry Arnold replied without looking up. They both proceeded to put their personal belongings into the small locker at the side of each bed as they absorbed the babble of noise in the long corrugated iron barrack room to which they and eight other conscripts had been directed.

Allan had reported to Budbrook Barracks in Warwick two hours earlier and after completing documentation had stood in line with fifty other recruits to be issued with bedding, uniform and toiletries, then with laden arms made his way to Hut No.5, his home for the next six months.

Allan was happy to join the army, it was the career he had looked forward to for years, he had ambitions to be an officer and stay in the army after the war, although at the beginning of 1943 the end of hostilities still seemed a long way ahead, but Allan was only 18 years old with a lifetime of hopes and expectations.

*"Stand by your beds!"* The booming voice of a sergeant produced an immediate deathly silence as the ten recruits stood to attention at the end of each bed, hardly daring to breathe as a six foot ramrod of a man, followed by a short, thin corporal slowly stopped at each bed and demanded the name of each recruit. Allan was at the far end of the barracks with his new friend Harry Arnold who was in line and due to be questioned first. Allan was shocked to hear the sergeant demand

of Harry, *"What tree did you fall from?"* Without blinking an eye. Harry politely replied, *"My name is Harry Arnold, I'm from Cardiff and I've been a boy soldier for three years Sergeant."* The sergeant did not reply, just looked long and hard into the eyes of Harry who returned the stare without a blink, then after receiving Allan's response the sergeant turned and without another word to anyone marched out leaving the weedy looking corporal to give instructions on the army system of bed making, cleaning, storing kit and a host of other rules and regulations. They were instructed to discard their civilian clothes, don their uniform and parade outside the hut to go to the Mess Hall.

*"Here, I'll show you,"* Harry moved over to Allan to help him into his uniform and show the correct way to wear his cap, there was an instant rapport between them and they sat together at a table to eat their first army meal of spam, beans, chips and a cup of tea. During the meal they talked about each other's family, background and aspirations. Harry was born into a large family living in Cardiff's slums, he had escaped by joining the army as a boy soldier and did not need to be at a basic training camp, but the army were making his life as tough as possible because of his ambition to become an officer. In 1943 there were very few black officers in the British Army, prejudice was rife and every black recruit had a hard time, but one with aspirations to become an officer was particularly targeted by the bullies and prejudiced of all ranks.

*"That comment by the sergeant was shocking,"* Allan said, *"Why don't you complain?"* Harry smiled, shook his head and replied, *"Allan, you do not complain in the army – ever, remember that, anyone with a rank higher than you is always, always right, never argue."*

*"But how can you take it and not flinch?"*

Harry laughed out loud and said, *"You're going to get your eyes opened, sunshine."*

Harry went on to give Allan an idea of life as a black man in Britain. *"At school we blacks had to go around in a gang for protection, but*
64

*fighting in Cardiff was our way of life and survival, at least two of my friends were stabbed to death, many others were injured and we were always targeted by the police so a police record was almost a badge of honour, only dockside jobs were available so I got out by joining the army as a boy soldier."*

*"Well at least you got away from a rough life, Harry." "Don't you believe it, you heard the sergeant today?"* Harry replied, *"Well that's only the beginning, believe me I know what to expect from NCO's officers and many others in this barracks." "But it's not right, how the hell do you cope?"* Allan asked with disbelief. *"I smile, stare into their eyes and try to be better than anyone else in everything I do, I expect to be picked on and bullied, I don't give them an excuse to go further."* Harry finished by saying with deep feeling, *"Allan, in spite of the bastards, I'll win".*

Harry was the first black man he had ever spoken to, all the boys at school were white and for Allan it was a revelation, he enjoyed Harry's lilting Welsh accent, was amazed at his sheer determination to succeed and couldn't comprehend how anyone could live with such daily persecution.

The following six months were the hardest of Allan's life, every bone in his body ached, he was tired of being shouted at from morning till night, and to collapse on his bed at night was sheer bliss. However, he slowly began to think and act like a soldier, his body was fitter than it had ever been, he could march in step on the parade ground and his accuracy with a rifle was as good as anyone. After six months he still found it difficult to get used to the language and coarseness of the majority of recruits, although he had become used to bad language at school this was in a different league and slowly he was dragged into their way of communication to avoid being a misfit.

Harold Arnold had none of the difficulties of Allan, because after three years as a boy soldier he was fit, could march in step, fire a rifle and obey orders to the letter. NCO's and officers gave him grudging respect and quietly admired the manner in which he responded to their racial abuse, his steadfast stare and enigmatic smile gave the impression he was mocking them, nothing they did could trigger a retaliation from Harry.

"I've seen it all before" Harry said, when Allan gave his commiserations, "I learned long ago how to handle those who hate black people, the odd time I've retaliated I've ended up with a bloody good beating and there's no fun in that."

After six months Allan and Harry looked, acted and felt like soldiers, following the passing out parade they were allowed out of camp on to the streets of Warwick, they were looking forward to being told of their future posting and regiment, they had both applied for officer training but were not very hopeful.

Next morning after breakfast all recruits made their way to the notice board to see their posting instructions, six had been selected for officer training, Allan and Harry were included, they were delighted but little did they know that a unique experience lay ahead.

# Chapter Thirteen

# An Officer and a Gentleman

The Officer Training Centre at Bedford was similar to the barracks Allan and Harry had recently vacated. They had met up after a two week leave, both were enthusiastic to begin training as future officers.

Harry's return home had been a never ending party of friends and family who were incredibly proud of his anticipated elevation to the rank of an officer. He would be the first black man from the docks of Cardiff to achieve such distinction and everyone wanted to shake his hand and buy the inevitable drink, even the girls were more affectionate, so with some reluctance Harry had to forsake his celebrity status and return to army training.

Allan's brief return to civilian life had been more subdued, lacked Harry's celebrations and seemed everlasting.

The visit to Aunt Sarah's was far from enjoyable, although she claimed she was unwell without specifying the cause, Allan felt a barrier between them that barred any long conversation as if his aunt did not want to indulge in any topic. His Uncle John hardly spoke a dozen words throughout the week, he had never felt close to him but their relationship was now almost non-existent, so with stinted goodbyes, Allan spent the second week of his leave at the school he had attended prior to army service, but even that was a disappointment and he arrived in Bedford with relief and excitement at the thought of his future prospects in the army.

To claim that Allan enjoyed the next six months of life is a major understatement.  He enjoyed every minute of his conversion into an officer and a gentleman in the British Army.

The tests and training he absorbed with a greater ease than his friend who faced abuse from two trainers who took every opportunity to highlight their opinion that a black officer would be a rarity in the army and would be a novelty to the troops but they stopped short of actual racial abuse, after all Harry may one day be their officer.

Allan and Harry were enjoying a rare evening out on the town mid-way through their training and Susan Robinson was having a girls' night out, with six of her friends to celebrate her twentieth birthday.  As the two young trainees entered the dance hall, Susan was suggesting to her friends that a dance at the other end of town may be more exciting.

The bar was crowded, Allan pushed past the girls to get a drink and apologised to a dark haired, brown eyed girl who simply smiled and acknowledged his apology.  Susan took little notice of Allan except to think to herself, 'at least he's got manners'.

After a drink Allan went over to Susan and asked for a dance.

*"We are thinking of going to another dance hall."*  Susan said, but relented and enjoyed the quick step with the young man she thought was good looking, had a friendly smile and had already indicated his good manners.

Susan and her friends never moved to the other dance hall, Allan was attentive for the whole evening, she enjoyed his conversation, humour and interest in her.  She was an only child living with her father who had been a widower for two years, Susan believed he would never come to terms with the loss of her mother following a car crash and even now had a feeling of guilt whenever enjoying a night out knowing her father would be sitting alone watching the clock for her return home at their agreed time.

Susan accepted Allan's invitation to the cinema the next night. He had a nice personality and seemed more mature than her previous boyfriends.

*"I'm going to marry her one day if she'll have me."* "Don't be stupid," Harry retorted when Allan made his surprise announcement as they made their way back to barracks. *"You know nothing about her, in any case we could move to anywhere in the future and she won't give you a second thought so forget it."*

Harry tried to bring his friend back to earth, after an enjoyable night out, but over the next three months the friendship of Susan and Allan blossomed, every spare minute was spent in each other's company. Her friends were abandoned and his time with Harry was confined to their time in the depot.

Susan described her life style, her family and that her father had been an ex-Palestinian Police Officer, attached to the army more than three years ago. Her likes, dislikes and passions were all conveyed to Allan during their constant meetings. In return Allan described his Aunt Sarah, Guardian Uncle John and his time at boarding school but refrained from discussing his childhood simply because his uncle had done such a good job on converting him to become a well educated English boy, all memories of his early years had vanished, well almost, in the back of his mind Allan felt that there was something he should know but Aunt Sarah would never answer his constant questions.

After a tremendous amount of hard work both Allan and Harry achieved their ambition and were offered a commission in the 'Royal Army Ordnance Corps'. With delight Harry invited his family to the passing-out parade, Allan's invitation to Aunt Sarah and Uncle John was declined due to their commitment elsewhere, but Allan was convinced it was an excuse. However Susan was delighted to attend, accompanied by her father who had accepted Allan into his home on a number of occasions and pleased to see his daughter so happy. Had he known they had spent a number of nights in a hotel it may have subdued his enthusiasm, because Susan was his whole life and no boy would ever be good enough, but he could see they were both deeply in love and so long as Susan was happy he was a contented father.

With pride, Susan watched Allan in the immaculately rehearsed passing-out parade, he looked so smart and handsome in the uniform of a second lieutenant for the first time, she knew that he was the one, even her father was impressed, he looked at Allan and recalled his own youth in uniform.

Harry's dark skin seemed to enhance his image in uniform, he was bursting with pride, surrounded by a family that were so pleased, all racial abuse and past intimidations were forgotten, Harry was an officer and a gentleman which was on a par with royalty so far as they were concerned.

Susan was well aware that Allan would face a posting elsewhere, her great hope was that the war would end soon, after all the successful 'D' day landings on the shores of France and the advances by the allied troops brought hope to the world that Nazi Germany would soon be defeated.

*"If only it could end before Allan got involved"* she pleaded in her evening prayers.

Allan and Harry could not wait, after all this was why they had volunteered, so they were utterly devastated to be informed that they were to receive six months special training in England. Susan was overjoyed, six months would see their relationship closer than ever, there was no doubt in her mind that Allan was the love of her life and one day would be her husband.

The two new second lieutenants were briefed by a major who said, *"You will both join up with a Captain and a Sergeant at a nearby ordnance depot where you will learn, store keeping, stock control and* stock transport. Any questions?"

"Sir, I didn't volunteer to learn about stocks, the war isn't over yet." Harry's voice was shaking with disappointment.

The Major had a smile when he replied, *"You don't know how lucky you are if you miss the bloody war, Lieutenant, I'm pleased to get out with only one leg so don't rush into the fighting."*

To emphasise his comment he gave his left tin leg a whack with his cane, and turned to Allan who said, *"What's the point sir, if it's special training where and why will we be involved in store keeping?"* *"Gentlemen I know no more than I've told you, so be ready to move out at 9.00 hours tomorrow, good luck, and report to Colonel Atkinson."*

# My Son The Enemy

# Chapter Fourteen
## The Truth - At Last

With tears rolling down his face, his body heaving with emotion, Allan stumbled from his Aunt Sarah's kitchen and out into the small patio, he needed fresh air into his lungs and to be completely alone, his life, world and even his sanity were in turmoil, the past two hours with his aunt had been the most traumatic in his twenty one years.

The year was now early 1946, war in Europe had been won. Hostilities ended and Allan had called on his Aunt Sarah to inform her he was being sent to Palestine prior to going to Cyprus where he would be involved with Jewish survivors of the concentration camps from Europe.

The special training of Allan and Harry had been intense and different to anything either of them had ever experienced. They had been taught stock control, stock rotation and sizing of all men's, women's and children's clothing, at the same time they were given a detailed explanation of their duties.

It was now known the full extent of the holocaust and extermination of millions of Jews by the Nazi Germans, but the number of survivors from concentration camps was unknown. However, it was almost certain that vast numbers would endeavour to reach Palestine (the promised land) and the British government was determined to control the influx by channelling the survivors into holding camps on the island of Cyprus until they could integrate them into Palestine in an orderly manner. Allan and Harry's destination was to be the town of

Famagusta where warehouses were in the process of being built to store clothing for men, women and children. Civilian labour would be recruited to work under the control of a detachment of 'The Royal Army Ordnance Corps' of which Allan and Harry would be officers commanded by Major James Armstrong. Although they had been trained and briefed they had no idea of the extent nor the magnitude of the task ahead of them.

It was with this background of information that Allan had visited his Aunt Sarah prior to joining a troopship at Liverpool for the journey to Egypt from where he would travel on to Palestine then to Cyprus.

His Aunt Sarah sat in silence as Allan told her his orders and destination, as he spoke he was aware that something was wrong, her face was ashen, her bottom lip trembling and he thought it was her reaction to him going abroad. When he began explaining his involvement with concentration camp survivors, she could not hold her emotions any longer. As if a dam had burst, her sobs and cries relieved an ache that had built up throughout the long six years of war.

Allan had rushed to hold and comfort his aunt with reassurance that he would be safe, the only word she repeated was ... *"No, No, No."*

For almost an hour she sobbed, her body shaking with emotion and held him so tightly it hurt. Eventually she calmed down and in a voice so quiet Allan could hardly hear she said, *"My darling boy, I must tell you the truth, it's long overdue."*

His Aunt Sarah then provided the answers to every question that Allan had raised over many years.

His birth in Nazi Germany, his Uncle John's determination to convert him into an English gentleman with false identity papers and the stark revelation that Allan was a German and a Jew. She had no idea of the fate of his mother and grandparents but suspected they had been sent to a concentration camp. His Uncle Albert and family had emigrated to Palestine before World War Two had been declared. She had been too afraid of John to tell Allan before now.

Allan sat in total silence listening to his aunt saying words that turned his world upside down, his mind in a whirl, it was difficult to comprehend her revelation but slowly the reality of his true identity became clear and without a word he rose from the kitchen seat, went out to the patio and sobbed, until not a drop of emotion remained in his body. His aunt had not moved from her chair, simply sat staring into space, relieved to have unburdened her soul at last, but she had passed an unbelievable dilemma to her beloved Allan.

He eventually returned to the kitchen and demanded more answers. The evening was turning to dusk by the time he was satisfied that every void in his life had been filled. He was a Jew and a German, a Jew and a German, over and over the phrase went through his mind. How could he come to terms with the fact after all the brainwashing, education and conversion his uncle had imposed on him for almost fifteen years?

Suddenly the door opened, and Allan took an almighty lunge at his Uncle John, he could have killed him without thought or compassion, he had never felt such hatred in his life. Aunt Sarah screamed, tried to get between them and fell down hurting her arm and lay on the floor sobbing uncontrollably.

*"What the hell do you think you are doing?"* his uncle shouted in a shocked voice as he pulled away from Allan and helped Sarah to her feet.

*"John, I've told Allan everything, he knows the truth,"* Sarah whimpered.

*"Why did you change me, you had no right?"* Allan demanded. *"I'm a*

*German Jew"* he continued.

John pulled a chair close to Allan, stared into his eyes and said with a snarl in his voice, *"I've had all records of your past eliminated, it was easy to do with my position in the Foreign Office, you are English and don't you forget it. I saved your miserable life by taking you in, you'd have ended up in a concentration camp, probably dead so don't shout in my house, in fact you can get out now."*

John pushed his chair back and without looking at Allan or Sarah walked upstairs muttering *"Bloody, ungrateful Jew boy".*

The silence was intense, only an occasional sob by his Aunt Sarah brought reality to the moment. Allan was in shock and complete turmoil. The story from Sarah had re-kindled a few childhood memories, but to accept his true nationality and religion was almost an impossible leap of reality in such a short period of time.

With a muttered *"Goodbye,"* ignoring her plea to stay, Allan left the house with a silent vow never to return. He made his way to a small park nearby and sat on a wooden bench. He must think, try to make sense of his situation and what should he do from now onwards.

Simon Schuman, born in Germany into a Jewish family was impossible for him to accept at that moment, and what of his mother and grandparents, were they still alive or had they perished in a concentration camp if all the stories were true about a holocaust?

*"Are you alright sir? This isn't a good place at 2 a.m."* A tall policeman brought Allan out of his thoughts and back to reality. He had been sitting there for three hours, not a soul around and he was bitterly cold.

*"Thank you officer, I'm alright,"* Allan replied and the policeman moved on.

Every detail of his situation had now been analysed and he concluded that he had two options. Go to his commanding officer, tell him the whole story, which would mean the end of his army career, and possibly more serious consequences with the civilian authorities. Tell his girl friend he was a German and a Jew could mean the end of their relationship, certainly her father would be a problem.

He could not get his mind around the fact that he was German, particularly after six years of war and to acknowledge he was a Jew was too big a stretch of his imagination – he didn't feel like a Jew.

Allan decided on his second option.

He would tell no one, he had too much to lose, he would continue to live a lie, after all his identity was secure, his uncle had ensured that fact, his family had most likely perished and he had no desire to see his aunt and uncle ever again.

All he had was the army and his beloved Susan, if continuing his identity deception was his price to pay to keep them, then so be it.

Liverpool and a troopship would be his next stop.

# Chapter Fifteen
# Middle East Problem

Allan's Uncle John arrived at his office next morning still seething at the audacity of the 'Jewish Brat' for being so ungrateful, if only he had refused to save him from the Nazis fourteen years ago there would be no pressure on him to ensure the boy's identity remained secure. If the press were to learn that he had used his influence to change a German Jew into a typical English boy, his career would be at an end and his hope for a seat in the House of Lords would be lost forever.

Within half an hour of sitting at his desk and enjoying his first cup of coffee of the day John embarked on the task that had dominated his life for the past two years – 'The Jewish Problem'.

As a senior civil servant in the foreign office he was considered to be the expert on the subject and relied upon by ministers to find a solution. Although John was a life-long anti-Semitic, his reputation depended on finding a solution, he was well aware of the persecution of the Jews and the historic background leading up to their present situation.

At the end of World War One, Britain took control of Palestine from the Turks, Jews were a tiny minority in the country and co-existing with the Arab with very few problems. John considered that Britain had done well in Palestine by building roads, schools, hospitals and even a university, however Palestine was the centre of a Middle East power struggle. At one time a so-called 'Sykes Picot Agreement' was designed to lay the foundation for a plan between England and France to divide the Middle East at some time in the future, however events beyond their control cancelled the plan.

In the early 1930's persecution of the Jews in Germany escalated, slowly but surely the balance between Jews and Arabs changed dramatically. With financial support from American Jews, a so-called army of defence called 'Haganna' was created, an intelligence network put into operation and arms poured into the country for future use.

At the declaration of World War Two, Jews had been encouraged to fight the Germans which was ideal for 'Haganna' to have their members legally trained as soldiers by the British (in one week 150,000 Jews signed up).

The Arabs took the side of the Germans.

John had proposed restricting refugees entry into Palestine even though, long before the end of the war it was known in government circles that concentration camps existed and mass exterminations were being conducted by the Nazis, Jews were even being used as bargaining tools by senior Nazis and John always advised against positive action. An offer to exchange Hungarian Jews for trucks was rejected, John forecast that thousands of Jews would flood the shores of Britain, it was tried to organise an exchange of Jews for currency via Switzerland and it was well known that Himmler intended to use important Jews as hostages to ensure his own safety if Germany lost the war.

However, the Foreign Secretary had given John the task of producing a solution to the Jewish problem that would inevitably occur at the end of the war.

Intelligence had confirmed the locations of a multitude of concentration camps throughout Europe with the possibility of thousands of survivors heading for Palestine immediately they were liberated.

British forces could not possibly handle such an influx of Jews into

Palestine at the end of the war unless there was some degree of entry control.

John and his colleagues had found a solution, and although it was criticised by some members of the cabinet as inhumane, it was accepted because there was no viable alternative.

The island of Cyprus was near to Palestine and under the control of Britain. The plan was simple, fortified camps would be set up on the island and everyone trying to enter Palestine would be refused entry, transported to Cyprus and interned in the camps until their entry into the promised land could be conducted in an orderly manner.

The practicalities of the operation was a relatively simple task for the military planners, but the humanitarian reaction and effect on survivors who had suffered six years of horror in Nazi concentration camps only to find that their liberators were forcibly detaining them behind high barbed wire fencing was not even discussed.

John's plan was already going ahead but he had not anticipated that the 'Jewish Brat' would be heading for the cauldron of anguish, heartache and sheer hatred.

Allan was unaware that his uncle was the architect of the hell-hole to which he was heading.

My Son The Enemy

# Chapter Sixteen
# A Jewish Terrorist

Albert Weisman, his wife Hannah with their two children, Trudi and Magdalan arrived at Haifa in Palestine on the fourteenth of March 1933. It had been a hazardous and emotional journey, Albert and his wife were only too aware they may never see their families again.

Albert was overwhelmed by the final farewell with his father, mother and sister Irene, if only they had joined him to escape from Hitler, but his father was such a staunch, proud German who believed that his position and wealth would overcome all problems, it seemed doubtful that he would ever join the exodus of Jews from Germany.

In spite of the hurdles and obstacles they faced during the three weeks journey they arrived at the 'Promised Land' in reasonable condition and the hoard of jewels given to Albert by his father were safe and intact sewn into the teddy bears his two daughters had innocently clutched throughout the journey.

They were refugees in a strange country with an unknown future, having walked away from an affluent lifestyle and influential status in their community in Berlin, to now mingle with hundreds of similar frightened Jewish families.

It didn't take Albert very long to convert a few jewels into currency and obtain a modest two roomed apartment in the Jewish quarters on the outskirts of Haifa in the midst of some fanatical Zionists who believed beyond all doubt that Palestine was the rightful home of the Jews with no place for the Arab population.

The country had been controlled by the Turks until 1918 and was now under British rule.  In 1933 the increase of Jews from Germany was changing the population balance, no longer were they prepared to be the minority, living in Jewish ghettos, they had major ambitions to create their own residential areas and eventually their own state to be called Israel.  If their aims required the displacement of the Arabs who had occupied the land for decades so be it.  The Jews had no doubt, they had absolute entitlement, backed up by major financial support from wealthy Jews in America.

Albert's wife and children enjoyed the warm climate of Palestine but longed for their affluent life style in Germany; missed their family and friends but were anxious for their future.  Albert's father had been generous, but his gift of jewels had not unlimited value, how would they survive in the long term?  Would they even have a future if Hitler succeeded in his ambition for power and the elimination of Jews around the world?

For the next few months the family simply survived, keeping themselves almost isolated, only meeting neighbours at the synagogue with an occasional discussion with the Rabbi.  They explored the neighbourhood, went on occasional excursions to Jerusalem and other towns they'd only read about, never expecting to live so near. They were aware of the British soldiers on the streets, a huge British army camp nearby on Mount Carmel but life was peaceful, frugal and safe except for the oppressive black cloud of concern for families and friends back in their beloved Berlin.  Every day radio and newspaper stories painted stark images of constant intimidation, murder and deportment of German Jews; Albert and his wife feared the worst for their families.

Six months after arriving in Palestine Albert had a chance encounter with Jacob at a café in Haifa. Unknown to Albert it was no chance meeting, Jacob and his comrades had observed the refugee from

Berlin since his arrival and were now satisfied he could be an asset to their organisation, if he could be persuaded to join. Albert and his family had just celebrated 'Yom Kippur' the holiest day of the Jewish year, a Day of Atonement, when they must fast and pray all day, while Hannah cooked a meal Albert took a stroll to a local coffee house, to an encounter that would change his life for ever, into one of hatred, violence and blackmail.

A tall lean stranger walked up to the table and said, *"Good evening, my friend".*

Albert made no response because Jacob had spoken in Hebrew and although he had begun to learn the language it was too soon for Albert to fully understand.

Jacob smiled and said in German, *"I'm so sorry I thought you had learned our language, by now. May I join you for a coffee?"*

*"Of course, please sit down, my name is Albert Weisman".*

With a handshake, Jacob took the nearest chair and replied, *"My name is Jacob Oppenheimer, welcome to Haifa, I hope you and your family are settling into your new home."*

Albert didn't reply, he was apprehensive, wondering how the stranger knew he had a family and was a new arrival into the country.

Jacob Oppenheimer was thirty two years old, over six feet tall with a distinctive full beard, he was a man with a mission. He was a founder member of the 'Stern' gang, an underground movement committed to using all means available to rid Palestine of British and Arab interlopers from the land they believed was the rightful home of the Jews. Jacob was a man consumed by hatred of the Arabs in Palestine and the British rulers who seemed to favour the Arabs at the expense of the minority Jewish communities. In 1931, only twenty four months ago, a bomb had killed his beloved Ruth and their six month old baby daughter, Jacob had no doubt that a well known local Arab gang was responsible. He was now totally committed to freedom for the Jews even if it required giving his own life in the process. He was a loner, with no other family or friends, his family were all in Germany, probably in a concentration camp, Jacob had nothing else to lose except his life.

# Chapter Seventeen

## Palestine in Turmoil

*"Gentlemen, welcome to the island of Cyprus. You have an important duty ahead that at times may be traumatic and emotional, you have no responsibility for security or feeding, your sole duty is to provide clothing for the concentration camp survivors."*

Early 1946, Captain Harvey was briefing Lieutenant Allan Lambert, , Harry Arnold and Sergeant Major Tasker on their recent arrival at R.A.O.C, Depot, Famagusta.

*"You were trained back in the U.K."* he continued, *"so you should know your duties, I want no cock-ups, no panic stations, just a quiet life."*

Captain Harvey had already done his stint of soldiering in 1942 in the Italy campaign, was no lover of the Jews and now the war was over he resented drawing the short straw to command a little depot he considered to be of no importance in Cyprus.

*"Incidentally."* He finalised, *"we don't expect any newspaper reporters, in fact it's planned to keep them off the island, - but if any slip through, you will not give interviews, accept free drinks or allow them in the depot, is that abundantly clear, gentlemen?"*

*"Yes sir"* his audience responded in unison.

*"They won't get near to the bloody camps, that's for sure,"* he said, concluding the briefing.

The Royal Army Ordnance Corps Depot covered four acres of land on which six mammoth corrugated iron warehouses had been erected and already full of clothing of every size and description for men, women and children. Fifty lorries were parked like silent statues awaiting a driver sparking them into life. The southern part of the depot was allotted space for forty other ranks who were housed under canvas, a guard house, mess hut and a N.A.A.F.I. canteen.

Well away from all camp activity was the Sergeants' and Officers' quarters. A magnificent detached residence that provided individual rooms, civilian servants, luxurious dining and recreational facilities. The whole camp was encased into ten foot high barbed wire fence, search lights and armed soldiers.

The work of loading and unloading bales of clothing would be handled by civilian Cypriot labourers.

Everything was in place awaiting the arrival of the first influx of Jewish concentration camp survivors from Southern France having crossed the Mediterranean Sea.

Uncle John's planning back in London seemed to be successful - so far.

After the briefing Allan quietly returned to his room in the officers' quarters, he did not relieve Harry from duty for another two hours.

It was becoming an ever increasing habit for him to go off on his own, he lived and re-lived his last meeting with Aunt Sarah and although his decision to live a lie was in his opinion justified, he could not stop thinking of the reality that he was a German and a Jew. He could not stop looking at strangers, and thinking *'could he be a Jew?'*, and any information about the holocaust he devoured.

*"What has happened to my mother and grandparents?"* was beginning to overwhelm his thoughts, *"if he hadn't been sent to England as a boy, would he now be with them or even dead?"*

The very thought of seeing thousands of Jewish survivors was beginning to stir thoughts he didn't realise he had, could his mother and grandparents be among them, what would he do to find out, and if by some miracle they did arrive in a camp, what would he do?  After all, to the outside world he was a British army officer who was part of the group keeping them in captivity.

Since boarding the 'Durban Castle' troopship at Liverpool ten weeks ago, Allan's turmoil was escalating by the day, his friend Harry was beginning to notice frequent periods of his disappearances in spite of Allan's determined efforts to remain normal.

Susan was oblivious to Allan's turmoil, their letters to each other were amorous, happy and beginning to include firm plans for their future, a wedding was an unspoken certainty.

The journey on the 'Durban Castle' had been uneventful except for widespread sea sickness when they reached the Bay of Biscay.  The ship was full of troops destined for the Far East, Aden and Palestine. The war may have ended in Europe but other problems still continued throughout the world.  As the ship neared Port Said in Egypt all troops had been issued with light weight uniform and many, including Harry and Allan received a circular identification uniform badge depicting a 'camel in the desert.' They were now part of the M.E.L.F. (Middle Eastern Land Force).

After four weeks at Tel-El-Kabir transit camp situated in the desert to become acclimatised to the heat and flies, Harry and Allan were ordered to board a rickety old steam train full of soldiers who were destined for Palestine to fight the Jewish terrorist gangs, who were striving for independence.  The train took a tortuous full week to arrive at Haifa railway station to be greeted by a massive blast from an exploding bomb nearby and the news that an outbreak of cholera was the reason for the erection of black tents at every street corner to allow families to deposit their dead.

Transport from the station to the army camp on the top of Mount Carmel had been by army trucks and everyone was lying on the floor for fear of sniper fire, everyone was cursing the Jews, longing to retaliate as soon as possible. Allan remained silent.

Allan was unaware that his Uncle Albert and family lived only a few miles away in the town of Haifa and was now an active terrorist determined to get the British troops out of Palestine, and push the Palestinians out of the area that would one day be the State of Israel, his hatred for the British and Palestinians knew no bounds, there were no limits.

Harry and Allan had been transported by ferry boat away from the continuous violence in Palestine and were now installed in the tranquillity of a small supplies depot in Famagusta on the beautiful island of Cyprus.

Unknown to Allan his time on the island would be far from tranquil, he would face violence and blackmail and travel down a path he would not have thought possible when he had kissed Susan goodbye only three months ago. Unknown to him various strands of his young life would soon knit towards a common climax that would determine his future.

His birth in Berlin twenty years ago, his conversion into an English army officer, a Jewish terrorist for an uncle and the prospects of his mother surviving the holocaust, not forgetting the love of his life – Susan back in England were all pieces of the jigsaw of his young life that was only half of the total picture eventually to emerge over the next two years.

Dominating his every thought and action, Allan knew he had to face, and overcome the one thing he could not challenge, the stark fact that he was a Jew. Could he ever face the moment to go public with such a mind-blowing admission?

# Chapter Eighteen

# Murder of Children

At the time of Allan's brief stay in the army depot on the top of Mount Carmel in Palestine awaiting transport to the island of Cyprus he had been unaware that in less than a thirty minute car ride he could have visited Uncle Albert and his aunt. The same uncle who had tearfully hugged and kissed him goodbye on the Berlin railway station in 1930, on that day they were so close to each other, but now in 1945 their lifestyles were miles apart. If Allan had called to visit him dressed in a British army officer's uniform it is more than likely his uncle would have shot him out of hand and asked questions later.

Albert's conversion into a vicious terrorist could be traced back to 1933 and his first meeting with Jacob Oppenheimer at a coffee house in Haifa. Prior to that meeting Albert had been a quiet gentle family man, who observed the rituals of his Jewish faith, but was not deeply religious, he left that to his wife while he concentrated on running their jewellery business with his father back in Berlin.

The first meeting between Albert and Jacob had been no more than a pleasant chance meeting of two strangers, or so thought Albert; Jacob was friendly, pleasant and understanding of Albert's plight, took his address (even though he already knew it) and they parted an hour later with a promise from Jacob that he would try to get a job for his new friend from Germany.

Jacob Oppenheimer had travelled the same route from Germany to Palestine five years earlier than Albert. With no family ties Jacob was now a loner and a fanatical Zionist with an absolute belief that a 'promised land' for Jews was of right in Palestine, even though at the time of his arrival Jews were in the minority and the Arab majority lived a frugal life based around strict customs.

The Arab culture was centred around the village headman who was given full respect, visitors bowed and kissed his hand, was never called by his first name only *"Abu"* meaning *"Father"*. Words of respect were exchanged over a cup of Turkish coffee or a bitter Arabic coffee and mint tea., women met in a separate room and wore a long gown that reached the floor with a head cover. Hyenas, Jackals and Bedouin roamed the streets and the old fashioned dry farming with primitive tools hadn't changed for centuries.

A woman was subservient and obedient, produced meals and children, infant mortality was high, the birth of a boy was celebrated, but a girl was considered second class and any wife who could not produce at least one boy could be divorced. It was a quiet, peaceful and primitive way of life that suited both the Arabs and British occupying troops alike. However the Jews were not content and were demanding change, modernisation and recognition of their existence to the extent of planning the creation of their own State of Israel on the land that had been occupied by Arabs for centuries. If it resulted in evictions even death of some Palestinians, so be it. Jewish demands and conflicts were escalating, none more so than in Jerusalem itself where the Dome of the Rock was holy ground to Muslims from where the prophet Mohammed ascended into heaven and on the same spot was the remaining wall of the great Jewish temple, the Holy of Holy place where Jews prayed, wept for past glory and known as 'The Wailing Wall'.

Conflict, anguish, brutality, even death of Arabs, British and Jews was an inevitability.

Jacob Oppenheimer was in the vanguard of a movement committed to the rights of Jews in Palestine, he was a founder member of a terrorist gang of fanatics dedicated to the overthrow of British occupying forces and in the eviction of Arabs from land to be designated as Israel.

They planned to use all means available and became the infamous 'Stern Gang,' of which Jacob was responsible for recruitment and Albert Weisman was part of his list of potential new members.

Albert was persuaded to join the Stern Gang by the simple offer of employment in an administrative role, it had no direct contact with violence or even high ideals of Jewish independence and suited Albert to perfection, his only desire was to have a job, and a quiet life until one day he and his family could return to his beloved Germany, and hopefully resume their jewellery business.

October 14th 1937 was the turning point in Albert's life, he was ready to leave his office after a normal day's work when his friend Jacob entered with an ashen face, put an arm around Albert with the simple comment, *"I'm so sorry my friend, but you need to be strong."*

A minor skirmish between a group of Palestinians and British soldiers had erupted outside the school where Albert's two daughters attended. In the chaos a hand grenade had landed in the school playground killing seven children and a teacher, on hearing the news that her beloved daughters were among the dead Albert's wife suffered a massive heart attack and was lying in the local hospital fighting for her life.

Albert would never recover from his loss, the void in his life was filled with a hatred he would not have believed possible within one human being. Although his wife survived medically, she became a mental zombie constantly blaming Albert for bringing them to Palestine and blocking out the fact that if they had stayed in Berlin the Nazis would have forced them into a concentration camp, where they may all have died.

Jacob Oppenheimer realised that Albert would not wish to continue in an office, his hatred for both British and Palestinians could be an asset in their cause for freedom.

Albert Weisman would become a terrorist and a killer for the Stern Gang.

# Chapter Nineteen

## Survivors On The Way

Lieutenants Allan Lambert and Harry Arnold joined twenty other officers in a large hut outside a Jewish Detention Camp to be given a briefing prior to the first ships of Jewish concentration camp survivors arriving at Famagusta Harbour on the island of Cyprus.

Suddenly everyone jumped to attention as a Bridgadier flanked by half dozen senior officers burst into the hut.

*"Be seated gentlemen".*

Brigadier Thompson's quiet Oxford accent belied the steel and determination of the tall man who was in total control of the whole operation.

*"Gentlemen you will soon be involved in a major international operation, the likes of which is unique and unless handled with care, humanity and efficiency, could result in a major catastrophe, our intention is to provide you with background information, plans of the operation and progress to date."*

With these few words he sat down and nodded to a short well rounded Colonel who with a twitch of his ginger moustache, rose slowly to his feet, his eyes covered every officer in the room, then with an educated northern accent, opened his remarks with a comment that he knew would produce immediate attention.

*"War in Europe is over, but we are involved here in a war equally as serious, do not think this is a holiday island or a cushy number, what we*

could face is deadly serious, our dispute is with the Jews."

Allan Lambert could feel his heart thumping as the Colonel deliberately took a long pause to allow his opening remarks to sink in, before he then proceeded to give an historic and update briefing on Britain's conflict with the Jews in Palestine.

*"The 1930s was the beginning of the influx of Jews into Palestine from Europe due to Nazi persecution consequently the balance between Jews and Arabs changed dramatically. The old traditional life style of the Arabs was unacceptable to the Jews who had modern aspirations and the finance from America to achieve their demands, equally as important the Jews believed that the land was theirs of right, in spite of being occupied by the Arabs for generations. From mild skirmishes the conflict has developed into all out war, now that World War Two has ended, many Jewish men have returned to Palestine having fought on the side of the British and are well trained soldiers prepared to fight for their demands."*

Without a pause, the Colonel continued, *"To complicate the situation the whole of Palestine is under the control of Britain, and British troops are in the middle of the conflict, the Jews wanted the British out and the Arabs feared a blood bath immediately our forces leave."*

At this point the Colonel sat down and Brigadier Thompson slowly rose to his feet.

*"Gentlemen we will take a short break at this point. Before we bring your briefing up to date and explain our involvement in this bloody situation."*

Tea was served and Allan tried his best to appear normal but inwardly he was in turmoil, particularly when many of his fellow officers made bitter comments about the Jews and their treatment of the Arabs.

*"Right gentlemen, be seated and let's proceed."*

Silence quickly descended and the Colonel continued with his prepared dialogue.

*"Atrocities are occurring every day, British soldiers are being killed and abused by Jewish gangs who will do anything to get us out, Arabs are perpetrating atrocities against Jews who reciprocate in like manner. We've already had three sergeants hanged from lamp posts by the Jews, and the King David Hotel bombed, a whole village wiped out and any soldier caught can expect lashings and beating as a minimum atrocity. The problem is escalating by the day gentlemen and the possibility is that the terrorists may infiltrate here on to Cyprus, particularly when the first holocaust survivors arrive quite soon, consequently from this moment the whole island is being placed on full alert for possible terrorism and you could be prime targets."*

The silence was intense, not even a cough or a shuffle of feet from any officer brought reality to the meeting. Suddenly it dawned on everyone how the situation could envelop the whole island and each one of them in particular, their fears were to be heightened even further when the Brigadier slowly rose from his chair to provide the final phase of information to the twenty officers.

*"Gentlemen, you have some idea of the facts leading up to this dreadful situation in Palestine between the Jews and Arabs, however the situation will soon escalate to an even more serious level."*

The Brigadier paused for only a few seconds.

*"We are expecting at least 50,000 concentration camp survivors to arrive on the island within the next few weeks, as I speak, they are crossing the Mediterranean in any vessel that will float and after six years of horror you can imagine the state they are in."*

He continued, *"sadly they expect to be landed on Palestinian soil, but we can't handle such numbers in the midst of the carnage already being fought over there, consequently our navy have orders to divert every vessel here into Famagusta Harbour and that's when you take over."*

The Brigadier's voice and demeanour seemed to mellow as he

continued in a more subdued voice, *"These poor souls have endured unbelievable horror from the Nazis for six years, after the euphoria of release, they are now attempting to survive a sea crossing in some of the most ramshackle boats imaginable, and they are unaware that our navy will then intercept and escort them here to be penned into our detention camps with high barbed wire fences, gun turrets, search lights and armed soldiers."*

In an almost inaudible voice the Brigadier continued *"Gentlemen, no matter what your views of the Jewish terrorists I order you to show some compassion for these people who have nothing and will be traumatised when we force them into our camps for God knows how long."*

The Brigadier stood for what appeared to be an everlasting period of silence while he readjusted his thoughts and asserted his control as the officer in charge. He stiffened his back and said with a more authoritative voice, *"However, Gentlemen, our duty is to carry out the orders from our masters in London, we will be strict in implementing our duties, we will be alert for possible terrorist attacks and we will deal with any camp uprisings firmly. You all know your individual duties and responsibilities, so good luck."*

With that final flourish he and his entourage swept from the hut as abruptly as they had entered, leaving the audience to ponder his every word.

Allan left the hut in a hurry, sat outside, lit a cigarette and tried to think straight. Jews, Jews, Jews the very word had his head almost bursting, he did not want to get involved in the babble of voices back in the hut, ever since his aunt had divulged the secret that he was a Jew his thoughts were slowly escalating.

He could not even remember his mother's face yet she was now constantly on his mind, was she alive? Could it be conceivable she had survived the holocaust, and heading for Cyprus where he was in the very army that had orders to return all survivors into detention?

*"What the hell are you doing sitting out here?"*

Harry Arnold seemed annoyed that his friend hadn't stayed for the unofficial discussion with fellow officers.

*"You'd think you couldn't care less and God knows what we're facing."*

*"I've got a splitting headache"* was the only feeble excuse Allan could produce on the spur of the moment.

*"That's no excuse Allan, you've had a strange attitude for a few weeks, what the hell's wrong with you?"*

Harry was concerned, because Allan had become very reclusive recently, not the happy carefree friend he'd got used to. However Harry's outburst was to no avail, they travelled back to the depot in silence, Allan would love to unburden his soul to Harry but his secret was too immense and the consequence of disclosure far too disastrous.

They returned to the depot, and for the next few days both men were engrossed in double checking their orders, procedures and systems. To clothe a minimum 50,000 people who had nothing, it could be a logistical nightmare, but security and possible terrorist activity would be an added complication. Transport was overhauled, civilian labourers rehearsed in their duties and security checked in case Jewish terrorists infiltrated. It seemed as if the whole island of Cyprus was holding its breath awaiting the first boat load of survivors landing.

Meanwhile at the Detention Camp the K.S.L.I. (King Shropshire Light Infantry) were preparing as if World War Three was imminent, many were war weary World War Two veterans whose hatred for the Jews was fuelled for no other reason than their demob had been delayed. The new conscripts within their ranks hated the Jews because they were afraid to disagree with their battle hardy mentors and lack of experience had them scared for their future survival in a conflict that was an unknown dimension and ferocity.

Every day, information about the concentration camps, atrocity against the Jews by the Nazis and the sheer violence by Jews against British soldiers in Palestine was the main talking point in the officers' mess, everyone had an opinion, the sympathy for survivors was overshadowed by the brutality being perpetrated in Palestine. Even Harry Arnold had firm views, he was unsympathethic to the Jews which was a surprise to Allan because if anyone was aware of persecution it was his friend.

However their friendship was already under strain because of Allan's refusal to take sides or even discuss the Jewish problem, nor would he join the wave of paranoia sweeping the depot that a terrorist could be around every corner.

In reality, Allan's outward appearance of being a British officer doing his duty was a façade and he was finding it increasingly difficult to maintain the image. After their briefing, the imposition of full alert and the hatred of Jews by many officers and men had Allan dreading the first influx of survivors arriving because he didn't know how he'd react.

Allan Lambert was aware he couldn't ignore nor disown his heritage much longer, he was a German Jew by birth and all the anti-Jewish comments seemed to increase his feeling of Jewishness.

Letters home to his girl friend gave no hint of his turmoil, he still dreamed they would marry one day and be happy ever after, but a surprise letter would bring everything to a head within the next few days and his future would take a turn he wouldn't have believed possible.

# Chapter Twenty
# Life in the Camp

Tension rose throughout Cyprus when it was known the first boat full of survivors could arrive within days, Lieutenant Allan Lambert was in a dilemma wondering how he would react knowing that his Jewish ancestry may come to the fore by his manner or behaviour, particularly when he was aware that his mother could be on one of the boats (he couldn't accept that she had perished). He could not speak to anyone nor could he appear too interested in the lists of names of survivors, even if they were available, but he knew he could not avoid attempting to find out the truth, no matter what the consequences.

Little did Allan know that his mother had indeed survived the hell of Mauthausen concentration camp, and was at that moment sitting on the deck of a rusty old ferry boat, overloaded with survivors from several different camps and about to set sail from Southern France on a treacherous journey across the Mediterranean Sea to their promised land – Palestine.

The fact that the boat was unseaworthy with very little food or basic amenities on board was of no concern to Allan's mother, Irene. This was sheer unadulterated luxury. She was alive, free and could even contemplate a future, the fresh sea air was like drinking vintage champagne compared to camp life where the only air she had breathed was the permanent stench of corpses, her future prospects had been the inevitable gas chamber, and freedom would be death, but everything had mercifully changed.

May 16th 1945 had brought her back from the abyss when the Nazi guards together with the dreaded S.S. and Kapos had left the camps only a few hours prior to the arrival of their American liberators who with shock and horror had done their best for those survivors still alive. Those with any remaining strength knelt and kissed the feet of the young soldiers who found it difficult to comprehend the sight of dead bodies, dying people and the nauseating smell. Chocolate and rations were freely handed out but the starving bodies could not accept such incredible luxury, young children had never even seen such food and were cautious to even tasting.

On the long journey to the South of France via numerous staging depots the reality of liberation sank in.

Irene's permanent fear was replaced by hope, every day brought her back to normality, tears flowed as she thought of her dear father and mother. Both murdered by the Nazis but spared the long suffering she had endured.

Irene considered herself normal and on her way home at last, however her normality had been confined to her mind, because she was unaware that at the time of liberation she was two weeks from death, her body could take no more. She had simply spent every waking moment vacantly staring into space re-living the horror from which she'd survived, she was unable to communicate or feed herself. With incredible tenderness a young American medic had lifted her on to the first lorry leaving the camp, with instructions to the driver on how to keep her alive if possible. Six weeks later her health and mind had improved, she was in awe at the miracle of her survival, she was in the hands of people who cared for her and the hundreds of fellow survivors on the boat. Life was now so wonderful and hope was a luxury she had long ago abandoned.

The experience of Irene Schuman as an inmate of a Nazi concentration camp was marginally better than the millions of Jews who did not survive, but her treatment was so horrific, it is impossible to imagine her years of hell inflicted by other so called human beings.

On arrival at the camp her first hurdle for survival had been cleared by claiming that she was an expert jeweller, but within hours of being directed to the jewellery sorting hut her father had perished in the nearby gas chamber. Her initiation ceremony at the camp was to be stripped naked, shaved of all hair, then totally immersed in a huge bath of disinfectant followed by the issue of a striped dress and a pair of wooden clogs, she now looked identical to other inmates of Mauthausen concentration camp. They lived only so long as they could work, and the aim of their guards was to work or starve them to death. Irene worked long hours every day sorting out jewellery taken from the never ending line of Jews heading for the gas chambers, she was permanently hungry, bitterly cold in the winter and stifling hot in the summer.

Due to poor sanitary conditions all types of ailments existed with very little medical help and to be sent to the hospital usually ended with a visit to the gas chamber, consequently inmates did not complain, continued working and usually died a slower death.

Some watery soup, a loaf of bread between four inmates was the total food for a day, and fighting over a few scraps of food created the law of the jungle, refined and educated people were reduced to little more than animals in their desire to survive.

Those who could no longer fight, simply gave up, and the look in their eyes, the way they walked was the prelude to either throwing themselves on to the perimeter electrified fence or simply sitting down to await the end.

The S.S. selected certain prisoners to act as guards with the knowledge that if they did not perform their duties as instructed they would visit the gas chambers, consequently the 'Kapos' as they were called were feared as much as the German guards. They were brutal and on two occasions Irene was bundled into a special hut and raped by a group of Kapos, an experience that almost killed her.

The fear of death, the smell of death and the elimination of all remnants of human feeling had reduced Irene to a shuffling skeleton without hope or expectation. The sight of recently hanged inmates, and the mountains of corpses was now part of her life in a way that luxury, affluence and privilege had been automatically accepted in a life that was now long past and a fading memory, her life had no value, meaning or purpose and reminiscing about her husband, father, mother and dear little Simon was far too painful to bear.

Irene's day of liberation was unforgettable, everyone prepared for the inevitable roll call only to discover that the German guards and the Kapos had disappeared, everyone was in a daze not daring to move, when the camp gates opened and American soldiers stood in total disbelief, unable to comprehend the sights before them. Many inmates were beyond help, but those who could were treated with as much assistance as the Americans had at their disposal.

Later the American commander forced local Germans to visit the camp to see what had been perpetrated in their name, Irene was lifted on to a lorry for her first step towards freedom and return to good health. She could not wait for the boat to set sail and return her to some sort of normality. Maybe she would contact her brother when she arrived in Palestine and could it be possible her dear son Simon would return to her life at long last?

Irene's ordeal was far from over. She would continue to face anguish, despair and even hatred against her own son.

# Chapter Twenty One
## Plans For Blackmail

Allan's Uncle John headed the committee of civil servants who created the policy that affected the life and even death of hundreds of people (British, Jews and Arabs), sitting in their well appointed offices in London they followed a policy that the plan must be expedient for Britain, but even handed for everyone.

Politicians rarely queried their decisions because everyone was weary of war, Britain was almost bankrupt following World War Two and due to the religious implications between Jews and Arabs, the conflict was rarely allowed to receive British headline status on radio or press, many of the British public were unaware of the Palestinian war in spite of the fact that between 1945 and 1948, 90,000 British troops were deployed and almost 800 were killed, not to mention the unrecorded numbers injured and beaten up.

The troubles would become known in some quarters as the 'forgotten war' an epitaph that Sir John had meticulously planned, but he had also provided the ground work of a conflict that would continue for decades and at ever increasing levels of violence, the Middle East was in turmoil.

Allan's Uncle Albert, based in Palestine, was in the vanguard of almost every act of violence from 1946 to 1948, the British were his enemy, planning and implementing any action that would encourage the British to leave and allow a new Jewish state to be created was in his opinion fully justified. When news of Britain's plans to detain holocaust survivors in Cyprus was leaked Albert and his fellow terrorists were incensed with anger, their leader – Itzhak Shamir (a future Prime Minister) declared a no holds barred policy, violence increased to an even more vicious level, Britain counter-attacked by flooding the streets with troops, including the sixth Airborne Division, declaring a curfew thereby ensured carnage on both sides.

At the same time as the army briefing in Cyprus, a senior civil servant from the foreign office was on board a British destroyer to give naval officers a top secret briefing, Sir John and his masters were determined that no one would be in doubt as to the action to be taken against the survivors of the Nazis.

Sir Donald Peterson stood up, cleared his throat, viewed the mass of gold braid uniforms and with a voice full of authority said, *"Gentlemen, there is no need to take notes you will each be given your orders in writing as you leave. The information I will give you is too sensitive to end up in the wrong hands."*

This opening remark produced his anticipated response. The audience were alert and wondering what was coming next.

*"More than 50,000 refugees are heading towards Palestine and your job is to ensure that they do not put a foot on land. That instruction is non-negotiable gentlemen."*

Sir Donald was in full agreement with the order, he was in sympathy with Sir John Lambert's anti-semitic attitude.

*"If by any chance a refugee boat gets through your blockade the 'Atlit' camp near Haifa will be in operation by the Parachute Regiment who will detain and re-route most of the Jews to Cyprus."*

At this point Sir Donald paused to allow questions.

Captain Short from a British destroyer was the first of numerous questioners.

"*I assume we board any boat that refuses to comply and we're authorised to use force if necessary?*"

"*Yes, you will see your clearance in the written orders*" Sir Donald replied.

"*There will be a number of very sick people on board. How will they be handled?*" A young commander enquired.

"*No one is to be allowed off a boat*" Sir Donald responded abruptly, "*Everyone and I mean everyone must be refused entry into Palestine and diverted to Cyprus.*"

The questions continued for over an hour, primarily on operational queries, many senior naval officers were unhappy at the task ahead, to face holocaust survivors in such a manner was, in their opinion, far from humane, but they had no choice but to comply.

At the end of the meeting, the naval personnel, in near silence, collected written orders, returned to their ships to plan an operation that many officers deplored. They were ordered to face people who had endured years of horror under the Nazis, and use force if necessary to ensure they were diverted to Cyprus to face further incarceration in British camps. Unlike the Nazis there would be no brutality or death, everything would be basic but they would be fed, clothed and cared for, but locked up for an unspecified period of time.

This action by the British made Allan's uncle Albert and his friends even more ruthless in their determination to be rid of all British troops forever, and although they already had a small secret network of people based in Cyprus, it would be essential to plan as much disruption as possible on the island to create world wide attention towards Britain's action against the Jews.

"*It cannot be true!*"

Albert reacted to news that his nephew Simon was in Cyprus.

His section commander in the Stern gang put an arm on Albert's shoulder and said, *"There is no doubt, Albert, the information has been confirmed, your sister Sarah is alive and still living in London with her husband, Sir John Lambert, but your nephew Simon had had his name changed to Allan Lambert, he is an officer in the British army and based in Famagusta."*

Albert could hardly take in the news he'd just received, his nephew his enemy!

His thoughts were interrupted when he was given an order,

*"Albert we want you to go to Cyprus and make contact with your nephew."*

*"You want him killed?"* Albert replied with incredulity.

*"No, No, No. He could be more valuable to us alive than dead, but it will take all your persuasion to encourage him to remember he's a Jew and we need his inside knowledge and information of army plans on the island."*

*"What if I'm not successful?"* Albert replied in a quiet voice.

*"As a last resort tell him his mother is on one of the boats heading for Cyprus, and if he cooperates he will see her again otherwise they will never meet."*

*"My sister is alive?"* Albert almost shouted for delight but with a voice full of compassion Albert was told.

*"We don't know, but your nephew will think it's true. He's in the perfect situation to help, Albert, you must succeed."*

*"What if I don't?"*

The lack of response was enough for Albert to realise that his nephew must cooperate to live.

Albert made his way home with a feeling of utter sadness, since the death of his two daughters, he had been consumed by anger against the British and Palestinians, his marriage was in name only, he and his wife barely communicated, but this latest news re-kindled the heartache he had for his family, that anger had obliterated for so long.

Had his sister and parents survived the holocaust, was it possible they may one day be re-united and he could put the recent years of violence behind him?

He lay in bed that night with only one thought in his mind, how could his beloved little nephew Simon emerge fifteen years later with a new identity, new name and be a member of the British army.

Albert did not sleep or discuss his orders with his wife, she could not possibly understand that he was on his way to blackmail his nephew with a lie in order to obtain his cooperation.

Albert and Allan would come face to face within a few days somewhere on the island of Cyprus, the outcome would change both lives in a way neither expected.

My Son The Enemy

# Chapter Twenty Two
## Naval Intervention

The British Navy was now on stand-by, ready and able to carry out the orders of their civil service and pontifical masters in London, anchored off the coast of Palestine the ships involved included the 'Verulam', 'Chieftain', 'Chequers', 'Childers', and many more including sloops such as the 'Magpie'.

The combined exhibition of the might of Britain was awesome against an 'enemy' of old battered boats without defences, loaded with sick, malnutritioned and dying survivors of the Nazis concentration camps. (This was one encounter that Britain had no intention of losing.)

The plan was simple, a boat would be raided, ordered to alter course for Cyprus and be escorted safely into the harbour of Famagusta. Any ship's captain who dithered or refused, his boat would be stopped by the pincer movement of two British ships, a plank would be secured and a boarding party of naval personnel equipped with helmets, batons and shields would take control of the boat, (by force if necessary) and take it to Cyprus. The ambitions of Jewish survivors to put a foot on Palestine soil was doomed, it could be years before they were released from British detention camps.

At the opposite end of the Mediterranean Sea was an armada of boats of every size and condition from small tug boats in poor condition to major passenger ships such as 'The Door of Hope', and 'Star of David' that were hired by Jews in America. Every vessel was full to overflowing with Poles, French and orthodox Jews, survivors with no identity documents but with a great longing to see Palestine and begin a new life. The small boats were rusty, leaking, with the minimum of facilities and bunks in every inch of space.

The survivors were still suffering from their years of Nazis' treatment. Many had the permanent stare of the insane, children had rickets and jaundice, many could not smile and found it impossible to adjust to a new life, some could not believe that food would be available again tomorrow and the next day, consequently they could not stop eating and hoarding every scrap of food in sight. Many were unable to show any emotion, to laugh or cry was impossible. None were aware they were heading towards some of Britain's mightiest naval vessels, the British army and further detention in guarded camps. They had hailed Britain as their liberators from the Nazis, they would soon consider them as hated enemies.

Allan's mother had been directed on to a small ferry boat with a bunk on its deck and a blanket for warmth at night. She was still dressed in camp uniform, but her health was improving, she was enjoying the sea air, the stars at night and freedom, glorious freedom. She didn't mingle with many other passengers, she still had the feeling of suspicion and distrust of other human beings that many concentration camp victims had developed over the years, she spent hours within her own thoughts. More and more she tried to imagine her dear son, Simon, what would he look like? What sort of a life he'd had? Would they ever meet again? Sometimes she was elated with expectation, at other times she was in deep despair when thinking of her father and mother, and the past years of horror, but her one hope was that her son was healthy, happy and a typical Jewish young man.

Her journey across the Mediterranean was uneventful, with reasonably calm water, it was intensely cold at night, but compared to the concentration camp it was luxury. Eventually food became scarce and water was rationed but the long sea journey helped Irene to begin her slow progress to recovery. She developed a relationship with other passengers, exchanging experiences, family stories and hopes for the future. Other ships nearby were a permanent source of interest with cheers and arm waving whenever a vessel came near. The constant drone of a helicopter overhead was ignored, some thought it was for their safety, in fact it was British and relaying constant information on ship movements.

The first shock was horrific for the survivors who unexpectedly encountered mayhem as helmeted sailors with shields and batons took over their boat amid shouting and screaming. Some young Jewish men tried to fight when it was realised that they would be heading for further internment, but fists were no match for batons and a few cracked skulls soon quelled any uprising.

The majority of survivors were in such a state of shock they returned to the subservient stance that years under Nazi denomination had cultivated. They crouched down, hands covering heads awaiting their fate, their Nazi tormenters had been exchanged for British who would control their future movement, destination and very existence.

Some could not stop screaming, a few jumped overboard in a feeble attempt to escape and one or two who were already in a very weak state could not absorb the shocks and simply died within sight of their promised land. The boat was soon under the command of the British navy and heading for Famagusta in Cyprus.

Over the next few months the same scenario was re-enacted over and over again, some encounters were less violent, on other occasions it was a scene of pitched battle, some of the big ships were rammed to force compliance but the navy won the battle, thousands of concentration camp survivors were heading for Cyprus and imprisonment in British camps.

A passenger on one of the boats heading for Cyprus was Irene, mother and son had not seen each other for more than fifteen years, unless Allan succumbed to his uncle Albert's blackmail, they may never meet.

# Chapter Twenty Three
# Blackmail By Terrorists

Lieutenants Allan Lambert and Harry Arnold were enjoying their usual meal of pork chop and chips washed down with a bottle of Commanderie wine, they visited their favourite restaurant once a week as a change from the mess. They were aware that their reason for being on Cyprus would be realised within days, because the first boats full of survivors were only a few days away.

The camps were ready, with hundreds of tents already erected, cooking facilities available, and a well stocked medical centre ready for patients. In addition the search lights, gun turrets and armed soldiers were in place to ensure that security was paramount, no Jew would be allowed to escape.

Warehouses were at bursting point ready to provide the first civilian clothing that some survivors had seen for years, bedding, blankets, towels and a multitude of basic needs were waiting to be loaded on to lorries and delivered to the camps.

The concentration camp survivors would be provided with their every need – except freedom.

The evening meal had been up to normal standard, it was Allan's turn to pay the bill, the young Cypriot waitress approached the table with the change, which included a piece of paper. With surprise Allan opened it, stared in disbelief, made his apology to Harry and hurried back to his room, locked the door and read the note over and over again, with disbelief.

*"You are a German and a Jew.*

*Be at the 'ruins of Salamis' at noon tomorrow."*

The note was unsigned but it was a clear threat. After a sleepless night Allan had taken a Jeep, arrived at Salamis two hours before noon, sat thinking and smoking until the author of the note arrived.

*"Hello Simon."*

Allan jumped with shock. The voice had come from behind him without a sound or warning of approach. He turned to see a bronzed middle aged man, formally dressed, looking down at him from a boulder. Allan did not reply, his heart was thumping, wondering who the man was. How did he know his real name was Simon, but more important, what did he want?

*"You don't recognise me do you?" "Why should I, we've never met and why do you call me Simon?"*

*"I'm your Uncle Albert, and the last time I saw you was at Berlin railway station and you were a little boy called Simon."*

Allan looked in amazement, he could not remember his uncle after so many years, maybe it was a con man out to blackmail him, however his Uncle Albert talked and talked about family matters that were identical to the information his Aunt Sarah had supplied before he had left England, slowly and surely the childhood bond between nephew and uncle re-emerged, blossomed and exploded into floods of tears and hugs. At long last both men had discovered a family tie for which they had yearned for so long but feared it wouldn't happen.

Allan gave his uncle the whole story of life with Aunt Sarah and Uncle John, his conversion into an Englishman and the reason he had decided to live a lie.

Albert listened without interruption. He was very apprehensive as to the purpose of their meeting, love for his nephew could not divert him from his mission, the cause was more important than family and he did not know if his nephew's allegiance to Britain would overwhelm his Jewish heritage, but it was imperative that he could persuade him to join their fight, the risk would be enormous, but the penalty for failure for his nephew could be catastrophic.

Albert took over the conversation and provided Allan with information and his version of the situation in Palestine. He gave a sanitised explanation of his own personal activities in The Stern Gang and described their ultimate aim of creating a State for Jews to be called Israel. Slowly Albert led his nephew through the maze of conflict and Jewish persecution over so many years until he felt that Allan may be ready to listen and accept a proposal to help his fellow Jews.

*"Simon, you are a Jew, every member of your family is a Jew and we are in a fight for our own State of Israel, it's our right after so much persecution and you can help in a small way."*

Allan never uttered a word, waiting with apprehension to what was to follow.

*"We don't want you involved in any fighting, simply provide information at regular intervals on troop activity on the island, any major changes that you think would help our cause, no more than that. We simply want you to be our eyes on the inside of the military."*

Albert stopped and waited for some response from his young nephew and hoping his plea would not need to be more sinister.

*"You're asking me to betray the army, I'd be a traitor!"* Allan said with incredulity in his voice.

*"I could be sent to jail if I'm found out!"* Allan almost shouted to his uncle.

With a deep sigh Albert realised that his task would not be as simple as he had hoped. He moved close to his nephew, put an arm around his shoulder and said, *"You have no choice, son, the group I support in*

*Palestine aren't playing games, the stakes are too high."*

*"What do you mean by that?"* Allan replied, moving away from his uncle's side.

*"Firstly your mother, my sister, is on a boat heading this way, co-operate and you will be reunited, if you don't you will never see her again. Secondly your refusal would mean you would be a marked man from the moment we part today."*

The silence between uncle and nephew was intense until Allan in a quiet voice said, *"I could report you even though you are my uncle, at least I'd be in the clear."*

Albert fixed his eyes in a deadly stare and said, *"Fail to co-operate or report this conversation and you'll be dead within forty eight hours, I may be caught but there are people waiting for my reply who would act immediately if I fail to get you on our side."*

Albert then continued in a raised voice, *"for God's sake, you are a Jew, you're one of us, can't you see that!?"*

*"I'm no killer or traitor"* Allan replied.

They both fell silent for what seemed an age, Allan's mind was racing, the prospect of seeing his mother again was uppermost in his thoughts. He had no doubt that his uncle's threat was real, but to say he was one of them had a hollow ring to it, he could not think of himself as other than a British army officer, but he must think rationally.

*"Suppose I do as you ask, how will it work?"*

Albert knew he'd succeeded.

*"We'll find a spot here at Salamis, where we will drop a note listing our queries and you deposit your reply at agreed times, very simple, no one will be harmed."*

Allan fell silent, he was in deep trouble and aware that his uncle demanded an immediate reply. He still found it impossible to consider himself as a Jew and be part of their violence, but any hope of being re-united with his mother was overwhelming.

At the same time he was aware of the consequences if he was discovered providing information to the enemy. If he refused, his uncle had implied that his life was in danger, if he agreed he would be in constant danger of discovery, imprisonment and disgrace.

# My Son The Enemy

# Chapter Twenty Four
# First Ship Arrives

*"We have to be at dockside at 5 a.m. tomorrow,"* Allan informed Harry, when they met in the mess for dinner.

*"Yes, I know,"* Harry replied in a stilted voice. The relationship between the two men had cooled dramatically, Allan was not the open and friendly man he used to be, refused to discuss his problem, they were now simply fellow officers with a job to do. Harry had tired of trying to return to their carefree relationship, obviously Allan had something troubling him.

The first ship full of survivors was lying outside the harbour waiting for a suitable tide to enable it to dock safely next morning. No one knew what to expect, but Allan had the added concern because of his heritage and recent encounter with Uncle Albert.

Allan and Harry together with the Sergeants were ordered to board the ship as soon as it docked and make an estimate as to the numbers of men, women and children on board in order to send supplies to the camp once the Jews had settled in. No attempt would be made on size or preferences. Many people in the depot considered the Jews were fortunate being issued with free clothing of any kind, in fact one senior officer was overheard to say, *"It isn't a bloody fashion show."*

In spite of his apprehension, Allan was not prepared for the sight that greeted him the next morning. Four miles leading up to the harbour, at intervals of six feet apart fully armed soldiers of the Kings regiment were standing with officers and NCOs parading up and down their ranks, refusing access to anyone without a pass and giving every vehicle a close inspection. A sergeant sitting in the back of Allan's jeep whispered, *"You'd think World War three was about to break out, they're armed to the teeth."*

*"Sergeant, it could be fear of terrorists from Palestine spoiling their party,"* Harry answered.

*"It certainly can't be fear of the boat people"* Allan said, in almost a whisper.

The harbour appeared to be engrossed with more armed soldiers, standing shoulder to shoulder, lines of lorries waiting to transport human cargoes, military police in pressed uniform, with a white baton in their belt made certain that no one could be in doubt as to their authority.

*"I'm beginning to feel sorry for these poor souls when they come off the boat and see this lot,"* Harry whispered to Allan.

Their jeep was directed to the dockside to join a group of senior officers smoking and chatting as if it was a social occasion. There was not one word of sympathy for the Jews on board the old boat as it slowly docked, hatred for Jewish terrorists on the mainland, the fear of terrorist activity on the island and the nuisance of caring for thousands of Jews for God knows how long did not cultivate many sympathisers.

The first on board the boat were military police who searched for arms and bombs without success but all seemed visibly shaken as they came back on to the dockside.

*"Jesus Christ."* Sergeant Tasker hissed, as he accompanied Allan and the others to assess clothing needs, ahead of them was a sight from hell. The boat was overflowing with humanity, all dressed in rags or the striped uniform of the concentration camps, the clothes were covering living skeletons and socket eyes, all staring with a look of pure hatred.

No one moved or made a sound, their shock and anger at being told of their fate had subsided following their detention when stopped by the royal navy outside the Palestine coast. The short journey to Cyprus had reduced them to subservient prisoners of the British army. The silence from so many people was eerie, the smell of filth and death was nauseating. Allan and his team realised they had an impossible task as they precariously stepped over bodies lying all over the boat. Allan stopped and bent over an old man who appeared to be in deep distress, only to realise the poor soul had reached the end. He was dying, and no one was moving, they were so accustomed to death, one more was not a problem, he would join the other fifteen who had died on the journey. Allan knelt, cradled the man in his arms and cried with a deeper sadness than he had ever known. That was the moment he understood the anger and bitterness that was devouring his Uncle Albert, unknown to Allan the man he held in death was only forty years old, his wife and two children had died in the ovens, he had been a prisoner for four years of the Nazis but would not be facing imprisonment by the British.

Allan slowly stood, indicated they should all return to the depot and simply make a guess on quantities of clothing required. He could not face another second among his fellow Jews but he was now so pleased he had allowed his Uncle Albert to blackmail him into cooperating with the terrorists, if he was Jew so be it.

He would help in any way that would stop the barbarity he had just witnessed.

As Allan and his team returned to the depot the disembarkment of Jews on to lorries was completed without major incident other than the quiet sobbing of men, women and children, the occasional shriek from someone being forcibly lifted on to a lorry and the yell when someone tried to escape.

The majority of army officers and men were shocked and subdued at the sight of these pitiful people, but a minority shouted, and bullied those who did not move fast enough.

This was the first boat to dock at Famagusta harbour, full of survivors, over the following weeks the scene would be repeated over and over again sometimes with major violence from some of the young Jewish men, when hand to hand fighting broke out. Small boats, major vessels and thousand and thousand of concentration camp survivors came under British army control. All media reporting was strictly controlled and the majority of British citizens were unaware of the activity being carried out in their name against the Jews.

One of the boats had a lady whose life had gone from wealth and affluence, saw her father and mother killed. Survived the horror of a concentration camp, hated the Nazis with a passion and now had the same hatred for the British as they forced her to enter yet another camp. She longed to see her dear son but did not know that he was actually a British army officer billeted less than two miles away.

# Chapter Twenty Five

## Caught in the Act

The largest camp was four miles along the coast at Salamis, well away from civilians. The perimeter was surrounded by a ten feet high barbed wire fence, with viewing platforms at each corner to accommodate an armed soldier with a searchlight.

Armed soldiers would patrol outside the perimeter fence twenty four hours a day. Hundreds of tents were already erected in long straight lines, a cook house, washhouse and a variety of other amenities all stood silent and forlorn awaiting their new residents.

Similar to hundreds of others, Allan's mother developed a panic attack immediately she was forced to enter the high gates, all the mental progress she had made on the sea journey was undone within minutes, the barbed wire fence brought back memories and fears that broke her mental stability, she joined hundreds of women who insanely stared into space for twenty fours a day, children continually screamed without restraint and male inmates were so incensed with anger and hatred against the British they began planning a break out the minute the door of the camp clanged shut.

After the arrival of the first boat Allan complied with his Uncle Albert's demands, he had no doubt he was doing the right thing, his mother may be on one of the boats and he now felt such compassion for the Jewish survivors he believed he was justified in  helping in some small way. He quietly visited his favourite spot at the ruins of Salamis, collected a brief note which had been left by a courier at an agreed spot, and two days later placed his answer. He was amazed how trivial their demands were, without realising the terrorists were planning to slowly lead him into greater acts of treachery within a few weeks when all survivors had landed and the camps would be full to overflowing.

Allan made no mention in his letters home to his girl friend in England that he was a Jew, was beginning to feel as a Jew and was colluding with Jewish terrorists. He knew he would have a problem when they met on his next leave in six months time, but hoped he would convince her when she heard the full story, and how much he loved her.

*"Excuse me sir, you're required in the C.O's office immediately."*

A corporal saluted and delivered the message to Allan while he was having breakfast.

*"It's either trouble or promotion,"* his breakfast companion lightheartedly commented.

Allan finished his cup of tea, straightened his uniform and walked the short distance to his commanding officer, knocked on the door and entered.

Sitting at his desk Captain Harvey had a face like thunder, to his left sat Major Thompson of the S.I.B. (Special Investigation Branch) and in the corner of the room a scruffy middle aged civilian sat smoking a cigarette.

Allan entered the office, saluted, stood to attention and waited for what seemed to be an eternity, no one spoke, the silence was ominous.

*"Lieutenant, are you a bloody traitor?"*

Captain Harvey was not a man to mince his words and his look demanded a response. When Allan didn't answer immediately the commanding officer almost yelled, *"Well?"*

Major Thompson lightly put a hand on his fellow officer's shoulder and in a quiet voice said,

"Lieutenant, I am Major Thompson of the S.I.B. The gentleman in the corner is from M16. We have some serious allegations to put to you and you can give us your answers now or request a fellow officer be present on your behalf."

Allan was visibly shaking, his heart thumping, his legs like jelly, and his throat was so dry he could not speak. The man from M16 saw his distress, produced a chair and a glass of water then indicated that he sit down.

Before Allan could find his voice Major Thompson continued his dialogue while Allan's C.O. sat upright in his chair glaring directly into Allan's face, The M16 man continued smoking with a less antagonistic manner.

"Lieutenant, we have evidence that you met a known terrorist from the mainland and over the past few weeks you have passed information to a courier who in turn transferred your notes to a member of the Stern Gang. We have absolute proof that can send you to prison for a long time."

"You'd better have a bloody good answer son, because if you'd been with me in Italy I'd have shot you myself!"

Allan's C.O. was incensed with anger but the S.I.B. officer calmed him by quietly saying,

"Let's hear Lieutenant Lambert's explanation, and no more talk about shooting, Captain Harvey."

The room was enveloped in total silence with three pairs of eyes staring intently awaiting a reply.

Allan was panic stricken, he knew what he had done was wrong, the information he had passed on was trivial but treason! Even the word was ominous, with tears in his eyes and shaking voice he spoke for almost an hour without interruption, told his accusers everything, from his childhood in Berlin, his Uncle John's obliteration of his original identity, his great desire to become an army officer and finally the blackmailing from his uncle to commit 'treachery'. Nothing was omitted and Allan was almost collapsed in his chair at the end. However he felt so relieved as if he'd finally shed a huge burden from his shoulders.

Before the two uniformed officers could speak the M16 man displayed his seniority by standing up, approached Allan and instructed,

*"Lieutenant, you will accompany me to HQ Nicosia where you will be under house arrest in the officers quarters, you will speak to no one about this interview, is that clear?"*

In a whisper of a voice Allan replied, *"Yes Sir."*

The silent journey to Nicosia, three days confinement to the officers' quarters and the mental torment reduced Allan to almost collapse when an order came for him to report to Room 115 at 9 a.m. the following morning.

Allan was surprised to be confronted by only one person and received such an informal reception, he had attuned his mind to be prepared for a court martial.

*"Come in Lieutenant, have a seat, a cup of tea will soon arrive."*

Allan was shocked at the lack of formality from the man from M16 who had accompanied him to Nicosia. He was still dressed in the same suit but with a fresh shirt, he was now clean shaven which made him look much younger than three days ago.

*"You don't need to know my name and so far as you're concerned this conversation didn't happen, I'm sure you'll understand when we're finished."* An orderly knocked on the door, delivered a tea tray and departed without comment, Allan sat in silence totally perplexed.

*"You are in big trouble Lieutenant, a dishonourable discharge from the army could be the least of your problems, you have been stupid but we understand your motive and incredible situation."*

He stopped speaking long enough to have a drink of tea, motioned for Allan to do likewise then continued.

*"I've discussed your case at the highest level and am authorised to give you a way out Lieutenant."*

He paused looking intently at Allan, *"We have now confirmed everything you told us three days ago, your uncle who contacted you initially is back in Palestine and under observation. You are being controlled at a much higher level in the Stern Gang, they must have big plans for you my son."*

Allan could hardly speak he felt so apprehensive but managed to whisper, *"What will happen to my Uncle Albert?"*

*"He will be watched every minute of his life Lieutenant but he is no longer a problem for you."*

The tone of voice of the man from M16 hardened and became very serious.

*"I want you to listen carefully, your answer could affect the rest of your life. We want you to continue cooperating with the terrorists, receive their instructions and deposit the answer in the same way you've done for the past six weeks."*

Allan gasped with complete shock, until he heard the remainder of the statement.

*"The only difference will be that I will supply you with the answers, it will be your handwriting, they'll never be aware, if you accept my offer you could help to avoid terrorist activity here on the island, breakouts from the camps and save many lives. Play your part and everything possible will be done to locate your mother and when this bloody business is done you*

can either stay in the army or leave without a stain on your record."

Anticipating Allan's response the man from M16 continued, *"Refuse this offer and I'm afraid you wouldn't find the consequences very pleasant for the next few years."*

The man stood to his six feet six inches in height with a military bearing Allan had not previously noticed and said, *"I'll leave you alone to make your mind up but you won't be stupid and do a runner will you?"*

Allan had no intentions of leaving the room, however he would not have gone far past the armed guard outside the door.

Allan sat staring into his cup of cold tea, knowing that his fate would be decided within the next few minutes, the thought of serving a prison sentence and being branded a traitor was unthinkable, he would never see his mother (if she was alive) and there is no way that Susan would marry him. To betray his uncle and his new found Jewish allegiance did not seem to be an option but he could not think of an alternative to one or the other. He saw a major problem if his uncle and fellow terrorist ever discovered they were being given 'army' information and not from him. Their reprisal could be fatal and how much could he trust M16 with the dangerous game they wanted him to play. He must decide before the man returned, complete rejection was not an option, it was prison or a double treachery.

# Chapter Twenty Six
# An Ultimatum

Commander Mick Bewick was a security officer of twenty years experience in many theatres of conflict throughout the world, he had been in Palestine more than four years and responsible for frontier intelligence. Now that Cyprus was a possible terrorist threat he had transferred his centre for the control of fifteen agents to the island's capital of Nicosia. He had already set up a network on the island that fed him a tremendous amount of information which is how Allan's Uncle Albert had been observed landing for an early morning rendevous in a quiet cove at Larnaca. Rather than have him arrested, Commander Bewick decided to have him followed and when a British officer became involved it was obvious something serious was being planned. Allan's Uncle Albert was later allowed to return to Palestine by the same route but an agent followed his every move and gave a daily report.

Unknown to Allan the courier was the young waiter who was short of money, a supporter of the Jews, and now under twenty four hour surveillance. After a few weeks it was decided to pull Lieutenant Lambert in for questioning prior to arresting his uncle in Palestine and the young courier in Famagusta.

Allan's frank and detailed information at his interview changed the plans dramatically, Commander Bewick could see a wonderful opportunity for using the Lieutenant in counter intelligence. During the three days of Allan's detention the Commander had to: have

Allan's story verified, get authorisation for his plan and have Allan's
C.O. transferred because he hated the Lieutenant.

If these requirements were fulfilled then his only task was to
convince the Lieutenant to betray his Jewish terrorist friends, with all
the risk involved if the plan was discovered.

By the third day of Allan's detention, a team of M16 agents in England
had rapidly checked out his story. Aunt Sarah, school, girl friend and
his early army training, everything was exactly as he had disclosed to
Commander Bewick, but one last item required verification before
the Commander could face Allan for his reply to the proposal that he
became a counter intelligence agent, his Uncle John Lambert in the
Foreign Office could be a delicate interview.

*"John, can you spare a moment?"*

The senior civil servant had listened to the London based M16
officer's story, and was visibly shaken, and surprised knowing Sir John's
anti Jewish attitude.

*"Of course, I'll come immediately."*

Sir John Lambert was full of expectation, his plans for Jewish
survivors in Cyprus was going without a major problem and rumours
about the issue of honours had been circulating throughout the
Foreign Office for days. Today could be his long cherished elevation to
the House of Lords prior to retirement in six months time.

*"Please take a seat, the gentleman from M16 wishes to clear up an item
of concern."*

Sir John's boss had an unusually stern tone in his voice and indicated
a well dressed man at his side without giving his name. Without delay
or introduction the agent came directly to the point.

*"Sir John you have a nephew serving in the British army in Cyprus,
although he is known as Allan Lambert we have information that his real*

name is Simon Schuman.  He is a German Jew who was provided with *illegal and false identity documents obtained by you in 1930, he has continued this deception for fifteen years, throughout the war and for entry into our armed forces.  Have you any comments to these allegations Sir?"*

Sir John felt on the verge of collapse and said in a quiet whisper,

*"I was only helping a Jewish nephew get out of Germany and escape the Nazis."*

*"Are you accepting responsibility for the false papers and the deception?"*

*"Yes"* Sir John quietly replied.

*"But has something happened to the boy?"*

The M16 agent stood, looked at Sir John and continued,

*"I'm sorry Sir I'm not authorised to discuss the case any further.  At a later date you will be required to disclose your contact for obtaining false documents and details of any other illegal activities in which you were involved."*

With that bombshell for Sir John he left the two men alone, quietly closed the door and reported to Commander Bewick that he was clear to proceed with his plan.

Sir John and his boss sat in quiet contemplation for what seemed an age, each struggling to find the right words.

*"John, I don't know what's going on except you've admitted abusing your position for a Jewish boy, I thought you hated Jews!"*

Sir John replied in a voice he hardly recognised

*"It's a complicated story sir, I'd rather not go into it at the moment."*

With a sigh of genuine sadness his boss said, *"It's obvious there is more to come that you must deal with, but for the service it is paramount* we can't afford a scandal so I'm going to suggest you go home, apply for early retirement on health grounds and hope there are no more serious developments."

*"Am I in line for further honours Sir?"*

John's boss just looked without comment.

Within an hour he had cleared his desk, while at home his wife Sarah was reclining in a chair with a cup of tea, and reading a book. On his arrival he stopped, looked down at her and said, *"Bloody Jews, you should all be in hell,"* then stormed upstairs, banged his bedroom door shut and never spoke to his wife again.

Commander Bewick was free to proceed with his plan, Allan's C.O. was given a sudden posting back to England with his second in command taking his place, it now only required Lieutenant Lambert to see the light.

*"Well son, you've had time to think, is it to be a court martial or are you going to help me?"*

Commander Bewick adopted a fatherly figure attitude towards the young Lieutenant, when they met the next morning, the young man was obviously under stress and if he planned to cooperate it was essential he calm down, act normal and trust his every instruction. If they could fool the terrorists with misinformation it could save lives, avoid conflict and it wouldn't do Commander Mick Bewick's career prospects any harm.

*"I don't think I have a choice Sir,"* Allan replied in a resigned voice, *"I'm a Jew and my heart tells me I must help them as much as I can, but I couldn't face the dishonour and possible prison if I don't cooperate with you, so give me my orders."*

Mick Bewick briefly adopted a military attitude by ensuring that Allan understood there was no going back, he would sign 'The Official Secrets Act' and never ever be allowed to discuss the episode with anyone on penalty of prosecution.

With that out of the way, he re-adopted his fatherly manner and discussed the practicalities of the operation, Allan would receive instructions from the terrorists and Commander Bewick would provide the answer for Allan to reply in his own handwriting, otherwise he would do all his other duties as normal.

*"If anyone enquiries why you've been away simply say you had to clear up a family problem."*

The Commander stood up, shook Allan's hand and ended the interview by saying,

*"I am your only contact, no one else in Cyprus is aware of our plan, I'll always contact you, never ever attempt to contact me, that reduces the risk."*

He left the hut, Allan sat quietly wondering if his Uncle Albert's terrorist friends had a network of agents watching the army agents, and who were the most efficient? He was in the middle, and his life would depend on Commander Mick Bewick.

In view of so much intrigue, Allan began to wonder if his mother and he would ever meet again, maybe he should stop looking and concentrate on his own survival, he realised he was a pawn between the Jews and the army and neither side would place much value on his life.

My Son The Enemy

136

# Chapter Twenty Seven
## Visit To A Camp

*"Sergeant, I'm coming with you today, I haven't been up to the camps for a few weeks and I need a signature."*

*"Yes Sir, I'll get into the back of the lorry, you ride up front."*

Sergeant Tasker made way for Lieutenant Lambert to join the driver and they slowly drove to Salamis Camp to deliver six sewing machines and a mountain of multi-coloured material to allow the female detainees to make their own dresses instead of wearing the army issue.

More than six months had passed since Allan had agreed to cooperate with Commander Bewick from M16. The Commander had been so right, the demands for information from the terrorists had slowly escalated to include classified information, but a reply was always given in Allan's handwriting but created by the Commander. Allan prayed that the Jews in Palestine were being fooled otherwise his life was worthless.

It would soon be 1948, Allan should have gone to England on leave, but it had been cancelled by the Commander on the grounds that his contact with the terrorists was too valuable to be broken. Other than a few minor breakouts and the detention of some terrorists attempting to land on the island, the deception was a success, the terrorists had failed to get a foot hold on the island and Commander Bewick's superiors were delighted at the success of his plan of deception, Cyprus seemed to be secure in spite of the army detaining more than

50,000 concentration camp survivors behind barbed wire in a number of camps on the island.

Allan had worked hard at maintaining an image of normality, at times he felt certain he could not continue the deception much longer even though he knew he had no option, he was far beyond the point of no return.

He tried hard to maintain a good relationship with Harry but it was so difficult, he was certain that his friend was aware that something was going on, Allan would have given anything to unburden his soul but did not dare. His Uncle Albert had made no contact of any kind since the one and only meeting more than six months ago, Commander Bewick had been right when he said that higher members of the Stern Gang in Palestine had taken over the communication notes.

Allan's real concern was for his girl friend Susan back in England, he ached to hold her and she had been so disappointed when his leave had been cancelled, her letters were as affectionate as ever and it was obvious she still had thoughts of marriage, becoming an officer's wife and travelling the world with him. His letters to her continued on the same theme, even though he knew their relationship could fall apart when she eventually knew the truth. He longed to write a full confession of his life to her but did not dare because M16 could be censoring his mail. He could only wait and pray that the love of his life would stand by him after hearing his incredible story.

Allan was jerked back to reality the minute the lorry turned off the Salamis road to stop at the main camp gate. To be stopped by armed guards, checked by a Guard Commander and every inch of the lorry searched was expected, the security was as efficient as if the inmates were Nazi prisoners of war. The transformation of the thousands of concentration camp survivors had Allan standing in complete surprise and amazement.

*"They've got their own bit of Palestine in there now."*

The Guard Commander explained, seeing Allan's shocked expression.

*"I think they are supervising us now and just waiting their day to break out, because there are so many, we couldn't stop them all and they know it."*

*"What would you do if they had a mass break out?"* Allan queried.

*"If it were left to me they could all bugger off to Palestine now, I'm fed up, but some trigger happy kids would shoot a few Jews, there'd be pandemonium, I'd end up in the Glass House for failing to maintain security and a few years from now it would all be forgotten."*

With those few words of wisdom the Guard Commander instructed four armed soldiers to accompany the lorry, opened the huge camp gates and with a wave of his hand shouted

*"If you don't come out in a couple of days we'll come in to rescue you Lieutenant."*

As the lorry slowly made its way to a huge tent in the centre of the camp Allan was aware that the deliberate stare of hatred from every inmate was as intense as it had been on their arrival on the island, every British soldier was their enemy (including Lieutenant Allan Lambert).

However, every one in the camp now had a heavy tanned appearance and a confidence that was totally lacking on their arrival, although they were secured behind barbed wire they were no longer cowed and subservient prisoners, children were playing, groups were being taught a variety of subjects and in one corner of the camp a group of young Jews - men and women, were actually being trained on marching drill. A hive of activity of learning and army training was being conducted by qualified people who had infiltrated the hordes of survivors at the south of France, crossed the Mediterranean and entered the camp. Not only were the Jews fighting hard to force British troops out of Palestine, they had obviously planned well ahead to ensure the camp inmates were able to integrate in a positive manner with the population when they eventually were allowed into their promised land.

Allan felt a sense of optimism among the survivors, they were well fed, healthy with a purpose for the future which made him feel happier than he had felt since being first told he was one of them, - a Jew, but the hatred against him and the other soldiers shone from every face that looked their way, the majority deliberately turned their backs.

The tent to which Allan had been directed to deliver the dress material and six sewing machines was huge and provided space for fifty females to make, mend and alter clothing for men, women and children in the camp. They may be prisoners but they were fiercely independent, the Jews were now a well ordered, efficient group who had suffered enough from the Nazis and had no intention of succumbing to the British.

*"Who will provide a signature for these sewing machines?"*

Allan asked the first lady he saw as he entered the tent, in return all he received was a shrug of her shoulders as if she did not understand (even though she understood every word). A similar reaction was received from every lady he approached, as he turned to another table a dark haired lady sat with her head bowed almost into her lap, he touched her shoulder hoping for a more positive response, whereupon she leaped out of her chair, screamed and ran out of the tent, she could not bear to look at or even be touched by a British officer, her hatred was almost as intense as it had been for the Germans.

Irene Weisman had no idea that the British officer she hated and could not bear his touch was her beloved son – Simon.

*"Get these bloody machines back on the lorry, I've had enough,"* Allan shouted to Sergeant Tasker, whereupon a man appeared out of nowhere and said in a quiet voice *"Can I help you Sir?"*

A tall bronzed man with a smile approached Allan as if the army man was the intruder.

*"All I want is a bloody signature on this receipt and we'll get out of here."*

As the man held out his hand an horrendous scream pierced the air, the four armed soldiers cocked their rifles ready for action as if they were expecting trouble, bundled Allan into the lorry and moved as quickly as possible through the hordes of silent camp inmates, within seconds the huge camp gates clanged behind them, a receipt forgotten and Allan was visibly shaking.

*"You decided not to stay old boy,"* the Guard Commander said to Allan as he gave him a cup of tea.

*"What the hell happened?"* Allan said with shaking voice.

*"Lieutenant we have an incident every day of the week but this was more serious than usual, I constantly tell the perimeter guards to avoid being too close to the wire fence but today a young corporal strayed and had a metal tent peg plunged into his back."*

*"What do you do about it?"* Allan queried.

*"Not a lot we can do, some bloody fanatic would be lost among the crowd within seconds and we'll get no cooperation from that lot."*

The Camp Commander nodded to the hundreds of Jews as they silently stood staring through the barbed wire fence at the extra troops now surrounding the camp, rifles at the ready and prepared for action.

The image Allan had seen on his arrival was a facade, the animosity and hatred against the British was as intense in that camp as it was on the mainland of Palestine, it was a smouldering powder keg that would explode into uncontrolled violence if their British guards relaxed their vigilance for one second.

141

Allan returned to his quarters with a mind in turmoil, he had mentally adjusted to the knowledge that he was a Jew, his support for their fight for freedom was absolute and his feeling of sorrow at their treatment in the hands of the Nazis was beyond doubt, but today he had witnessed a side of their character that was ruthless, a young British soldier had been murdered in cold blood, without one Jew showing concern. Did the treatment of Jews by the Germans and the British give them automatic justification to perpetrate their own atrocities?

Allan was unhappy at the treatment he had received from the Jews when everything he had delivered had been for their benefit, it appeared there was no room for compromise. For the first time he questioned his future. Did he wish to continue his identity as a British Army officer with the name of Lambert, or revert to his true name of Simon Schuman, a German Jew and support their philosophy of life, death and retribution? For the first time he realised that he had a choice.

If he had known that the lady whose shoulder he had touched was his mother maybe his dilemma would have been more easily resolved.

# Chapter Twenty Eight
# A State Is Born

Commander Bewick's counter intelligence had succeeded far beyond his expectations, his plan was simple, he provided sufficient information that was true and could be verified by the terrorists, to hoodwink them into believing the majority of the answers to their queries to Lieutenant Lambert were equally dependable. In fact the British intelligence was always one step ahead and prevented terrorist activity on the island.

Allan's uncle Albert was no longer an active terrorist and a killer, he was now a member of the political elite who were planning the future for a new State to be called Israel. He was being rewarded for being the planner and perpetrator of some of the most notorious acts of violence all in the cause of freedom for the Jews. He was now being trained to use his skill without a weapon, with a smile on his face and a determination as ruthless as ever, he was a facilitator for his political masters.

Similar to so many terrorists who turned into politicians, Albert was able to publically ignore his past, but alone at night he found it impossible to erase memories, such as the carnage he had witnessed at an Arab village.

Albert had been sent by the leaders of the Stern Gang to be an observer to an action by terrorists to teach the Arabs a lesson. Before dawn on Friday April 9th 1948, 120 fighters from the Irgun and Stern Gangs embarked on a hot blooded massacre, old men, women and children, 168 were slaughtered from a village population of approximately 800, the village was left deserted and in ruins.

Albert was later involved as leader of one group evicting Palestinian families from their homes to free land that would be the future State of Israel. In a small village called Faice, a family of two brothers, two sisters and their parents were made homeless from the house they called home for almost twenty years, simply because their property was five metres on the wrong side of the proposed boundary line.

Albert was well aware that his action was being repeated all over Palestine and thousands of homeless families joined a stream of frightened people heading for Amman in Jordan. The torturous journey took them south of Jericho, through the Judean wilderness to the heat of the Jordan valley. After weeks of hunger, water shortage and sickness the survivors arrived at a tented United Nations Refugee Camp on the outskirts of Amman that would be their future home.

They were part of the human cost involved in the creation of the new State of Israel, and at the time Albert believed he was fully justified in any action towards the cause for a Jewish State.

As Albert grew older he was finding it difficult to forget such scenes and many more from his mind, since the death of his two beloved children his life had been dedicated to killing as many Arabs and British soldiers as possible, he was now beginning to question his actions and wonder what life was all about, he was forty six years old, the relationship with his wife Hannah had marginally improved but would have collapsed completely if she had had the slightest inkling of his past few years of violence.

He was concerned at the danger he had put his nephew in but to all accounts everyone was satisfied and considered Allan to be a loyal supporter in their cause.

From the secret lists of survivors in the camps, Albert had learned that his sister Irene was alive and well in the Salamis Camp on Cyprus, but he had been refused permission to notify Lieutenant Lambert that his mother was alive, they were afraid he would try to do something stupid, contact her, and thereby endanger their conspiracy, Albert could not find any news about his father and mother.

*"Gentlemen, please be seated, today is the most momentous of our lives, what I have to say is top secret and must not be repeated even to your families, they will hear the news soon enough."*

Albert was a junior member of a group of twenty high profile people sitting at a huge table in a house in Jerusalem. He had been invited to listen, observe but not become involved, however Albert was well aware that politically their fight for freedom was now on the world agenda. On November 29th 1947 the United Nations had voted for the partition of Palestine and the creation of a Jewish State, British rule was hated by everyone and at last the idea of State for Jewish people had been internationally accepted.

That night the Jews celebrated and danced in the streets, the Arabs in Jerusalem and other cities rioted, looted stores and set them on fire, while British troops remained independent.

It was now March 1948 and the man who opened the meeting had Albert mesmerised simply by being in the same room as such a dynamic and charismatic leader of the Jews.

David Ben Gurion, sixty two years old, and destined to be the first Prime Minister of the first Jewish State, he was a white haired vibrant man born in 1886 in Plonsk, Russia and had dedicated his life to creating a State for the Jews in Palestine. By the age of fourteen he had established a Zionist Youth Society, he did farm work on a Jewish settlement, he edited a Zionist Workers Hebrew Language Newspaper but was expelled from Palestine by the Turks and arrived in New York in 1915.

His hope for a Jewish State was revived with the British 'Balfour Declaration' in 1917, in return Ben Gurion helped to organise a Jewish Legion for the British forces during the war. On his eventual return to Palestine he was to discover the British were in absolute control but he still managed to become General Secretary of 'Histadrut' a confederation of Jewish workers, he formed the Zionist Labour Party and in 1935 he became the Chairman of the Agency for overseeing the Jews in the Holy Land.

Ben Gurion was a man who was creating a State within a State, and when Britain restricted Jewish immigration into Palestine the ground was already prepared for the beginning of sabotage and terrorist attacks, all authorised by the man that Albert was now watching with awe, the man considered to be the father of his country and the hero of almost every Jew on earth.

In total silence Albert and the other members of the audience heard with disbelief David Ben Gurion inform them that within a few weeks, on May 14th 1948 the British forces would leave Palestine forever, Camps in Cyprus would be closed down and the new State for Jews to be called 'Israel' would be created. After a few seconds of breathless silence the room erupted into shouting, tears and embraces, the long fight was over and they had defeated the British.

Ben Gurion allowed the euphoria to subside and then brought everyone back to earth.

*"Gentlemen, our fight for survival is only now beginning, the Arab States will never accept our existence and immediately the British pull out we will be at war."*

Albert was utterly demoralised at the news, little did he realise that sixty years later, and in spite of major achievements over the years by the State of Israel they would still be fighting for survival and the right to live in peace.

However the immediate task was to unite all the different Gangs in a common cause against the Arab States who were under the command of a former British Army officer called John Glubb and known as 'Glubb Pasha'.

Against all odds the Arab States were defeated, Jews could now build a State that would survive in spite of repeated attacks from all Arab quarters.

Albert was tired of killing, weary of hatred and longed to unite his family in peace as they had been so long ago in Berlin before Hitler had taken control of Germany. He still had most of the jewels his father had given and he had been well paid by the Stern Gang for his services, but where could he find peace and tranquillity?

Ben Gurion's statement that the fight for survival was only just beginning was devastating for Albert, his hope that Britain's departure would bring peace was thinking against reality. The Arabs had been evicted from their land, persecuted and ethnic cleansed, they would never forgive or forget. Thousands of Jews had been condemned to an extra two years detention by the British in addition to hundreds of Jewish killings by British forces since 1945, Britain would always be viewed with suspicion by future generations, Germany would never be forgiven.

Jews had faced unbelievable horrors and persecution that brought justified sympathy world wide but their ruthless actions in retaliation had revived anti-semitic feelings in many parts of the world that insured peace would be as elusive as ever. In addition opposing factions between the Jews themselves on which direction the new State of Israel should take created internal battles.

Albert's need and desire for a life of peace and reconciliation with his own conscience would be difficult to achieve, but he was determined that somewhere he would find a haven for him and those members of his family who had survived.

# My Son The Enemy

*friendship because I am truly very sorry."*

Allan then told his friend the whole story about his life, his early days in Berlin, the deception created by his uncle in England, his blackmail by terrorists and the army's counter blackmail.

*"Incidentally Harry if you mention a word of this to anyone I will end up in jail because I had to sign the Official Secrets Act."*

Harry stayed silent as they continued a slow walk around the perimeter of the camp.

*"For God's sake say something!"* Allan said in a quiet voice.

Harry stopped, looked directly at Allan and said, *"I don't give a damn whether you're a German and a Jew Allan, even though I admit I'm no lover of the Jews, many have suffered, but my God they're ruthless, particularly against the Palestinians, and you don't need me to tell you how much I hate the bloody Germans. But none of this is your fault Allan, although if I'd found out about your background from someone else I'd probably have added you to my hate list."*

Harry held out his hand to Allan their friendship seemed to be back on course and he ended their conversation by saying,

*"I'm not going home for another month, we must keep in touch and you know you have a big decision to make, are you going to remain an Englishman or will you be a German and a Jew?"*

Although they parted with a smile and a firm handshake Allan sensed that Harry now looked at him as a German and a Jew.

*"Thank God I'm going home"* Allan muttered to himself, but where was home? If Susan had the same reaction as Harry they would have no future together, he could not face going to his Aunt Sarah and he would never set eyes on his Uncle John again as long as he lived. His mother was in Israel, he was not allowed into the country, had no idea how they would ever meet, and she may even hate him, when she

knew he was in the British army.

On his moments of depression during the slow journey home on the 'Durban Castle' troopship Allan could see no bright light of a future for himself. Even if Susan initially accepted him she may have future doubts, would she accept what family of his remained? Would they accept her? And God knows what her father's reaction would be. To be a German in 1948 was bad enough, to admit he was also a Jew could be a hurdle too far.

The ship docked in Southampton, where Allan was given his pay and authorisation for four weeks leave, he boarded a train for what seemed the longest journey of his life, all the past trials and tribulations were behind him, Harry and he would never meet again, Susan's reaction would determine the future direction of his life, his nationality, religion and even his happiness or dejection.

# Chapter Thirty
# Reunion In England

Allan's mother was one of the last of the passengers to disembark from the ship that had transported the first allocation of inmates from the British Detention Camp, she had held back to allow others to rush on to their promised land, she was in no hurry to face the unknown. Now forty eight years old, she looked twenty years older and felt that her life had no future, she had a permanent stoop and a slight limp due to severe frostbite four years earlier, she was arriving in a new country, and knew no one. Her brother Albert, his wife and children had travelled to Palestine before she and her parents had been deported but it was unlikely that they would meet, she had no idea where to look for him. At least in the camp they had been well fed, and there was some degree of organisation even though they were prisoners. She slowly walked down the ship's gangplank feeling so alone and fearful for her future, freedom was wonderful but it was accompanied by uncertainty and responsibility, a situation she had not faced since those wonderful days when her whole family lived together in wealth and luxury, - her whole family, she mused included her dear son Simon, it was too painful even to think of him.

*"Irene! Irene!"*

She did not look up, she was a number, no one had uttered her name for years, but as she reached the dock side a man and woman rushed to embrace her, she cowered as if to return to the ship until the voice said, *"Irene, it's Albert and Hannah."*

She slowly lifted her head and there he was, her beloved brother, if he had not held her so tightly she would have collapsed, the three of them cried and embraced each other for an age, as if their meeting was an illusion and to cease contact would have been the disintegration of the most wonderful moment of their lives.

Albert slowly guided his wife and sister to an awaiting car, he was shocked at Irene's appearance, her face was so lined and etched with the horrors she had suffered, no longer the happy, vivacious dark haired beauty of his memory, she was now an old woman who needed all the love and care he could give. He hoped that Hannah would develop a happier disposition at the sight of Irene, maybe this homecoming could be a saviour for them all.

For a long time they delayed asking each other questions, fearful of the answers. Irene was installed in the first comfortable room she had seen since being deported and wondered if she could sleep in such a comfortable bed, the meal was sumptuous but far beyond Irene's digestive capabilities, but they were happy, so blissfully happy, no one wanted to break the magic of the moment by questions.

Irene suddenly took her brother's hand and whispered *"Our parents are dead!"*

Irene had no tears left to shed but Albert and his wife were inconsolable when they learned the horrific details. Although he suspected his parents had perished, Albert found it hard to believe that such brutality had been performed against his parents.

However, it put into clear focus the acts of violence and brutality he had perpetrated against Arabs and British soldiers, but he had not known his victims, they were faceless, this was his mother and father he had just learned about.

Well into the early hours they talked with continuous breaks to allow tears to subside, Irene learned about the deaths of Albert's children, the long fight for freedom and the victorious new Jewish State of Israel. Irene said very little about the concentration camps and her life under the Nazis, 'Maybe one day' she said, *"but not now."* Irene was desperate for news of her dear Simon, Hannah made a fresh pot of coffee and Albert told her the full story of her son as it had been related to him in Cyprus, he left nothing out including his orders to blackmail Allan to secure his cooperation.

For a long time Irene was silent, quietly weeping her first tears for years, whilst Albert sat with his arms around her shoulders trying to give some strength. Eventually the tears ceased to flow, her heaving shoulders calmed and she sat silent, absorbing the information Albert had given her. Her son converted to an Englishman, with a new name, now an officer in the British Army, actively involved in the very camp in which she'd been detained and wearing the uniform she hated.

She slowly lifted her head, gave Albert a kiss on the cheek and said,

*"He's alive, that's the most important thing, I don't care about anything else, what's happened in the past has gone, I want no more anger, bitterness, recriminations or even hate, Albert, my body and mind can take no more, all I want is to live what life I have left in peace and quiet."*

He gave his sister a hug and simply said, *"I understand."*

Albert understood in a way Irene would never believe because he would not divulge to a living soul his activities since his daughters were killed. He had been consumed by absolute hatred against Arabs and British alike, life had no meaning for him and there was no shortage of fellow terrorists willing to fuel his hatred. Their aim for a new State of Israel had been achieved, but it seemed the fight was only beginning and like his sister Albert could take no more hatred and violence, his great desire was to make up for the years he had neglected his wife at her hour of sadness, he longed to rekindle their loving relationship if only she would allow him.

Over the following weeks Albert and Hannah devoted their time helping Irene to recuperate with good food, company and sightseeing. Visits to the synagogue were wonderful for Irene after such a long lapse in celebrating her faith, she was greeted with warmth and compassion by everyone and every day produced an improvement in her health, confidence and love of life, she and Albert's wife became as close as sisters, they both benefited from each other's company.

Albert was unable to make contact with Allan but he wrote a letter to sister Sarah with the good news about Irene and proposing the idea of a family reunion somehow, somewhere. Albert and his wife were slowly becoming closer, Hannah had known all along about his terrorist activities, but was not concerned about anything in life following the loss of her beautiful daughters. Although Palestine (now Israel) had been their life saver when fleeing the Nazis, Albert believed he had repaid his debt many, many times over and would dearly like to move on, but to where?

A letter from sister Sarah opened a door by inviting them to England for a long holiday. She had divorced her husband and her lawyer had negotiated a good financial settlement, (much to John's anger). Germany was too demolished for her to consider immediately returning, in any case she had no one to return to and although England was in the throes of post-war austerity she had become comfortable in living style and culture.

Now living in a beautiful part of Derbyshire, she had a cottage at Matlock and would love to see them if they could make the journey, and in the meantime she would try to contact Irene's son.

When Albert told his wife and sister of Sarah's proposal, Hannah was overjoyed to leave Israel and the continuous fighting with the Palestinians, Irene was apprehensive about Britain, she still considered them an enemy of the Jews, but her fears took second place at the prospect of seeing her son once more.

Albert applied for a long leave of absence on compassionate grounds, then used every contact, pulled in every favour in order to obtain travel documents, they would soon be heading for England and a reunion beyond their wildest dreams.

My Son The Enemy

# Chapter Thirty One
## Wedding Plans

With trepidation and a heart beating like a drum Allan knocked on Susan's door, she flung herself into his arms with a squeal of delight, kissed and hugged him with such enthusiasm he wished to God he could spare her the anguish he was about to impose. He loved her so much the thought of them parting was too hard to bear, but he knew he could not avoid opening his heart telling her his true identity and praying it would not change their love for each other.

Susan was full of chatter about anything and everything, she was so excited at having Allan with her she could not stop talking, serving his favourite meal was delayed because every time she passed his seat was an excuse for a passionate kiss and a cuddle.

Allan listened while Susan explained that she was now living in the house on her own, her father was permanently in a care home living in a world of his own with dementia, he did not even recognise her. She worked at a local estate agent and her long time girl friends ensured she had a reasonable social life, but now Allan was home she was content and could not wait to finish the meal.

Although hungry he had difficulty digesting and showing enthusiasm for Susan's cooking, eventually they were sitting together in a big armchair enjoying an after dinner glass of wine, Susan on his knee, her head on his shoulder, Allan took a deep breath and said in a quiet voice, *"Darling, I have something important to say to you."* His tone of voice made Susan sit up straight.

*"You're going abroad again?"* she said with anxiety in her voice.

*"No, my love, it's much more complex than that."*

For the next hour Allan told Susan the true story of his life, a story he had rehearsed over and over again. Occasionally she gasped and at other times she cried uncontrollably, all the time she edged away from him until by the time he had finished telling her of being blackmailed by his uncle and the army she was sitting at his feet taking in every word without comment or interruption.

Finally Allan had exhausted every piece of information he had, the only sound was the crackle of the fire and the tick of the large clock in the hall, Susan was motionless and silently crying.

After an eternity of deathly silence, and with heartbreaking sadness Allan whispered,

*"Do you want me to leave?"*

Ominously Susan did not answer immediately, then with a broken voice she said, *"Allan, I cannot absorb everything so quickly, please do not press me for an immediate reply, I need to become adjusted to everything you've just told me."*

*"Is it because I'm a Jew or that I'm a German or both?"* Allan asked.

*"I don't know, to me you're Allan Lambert and I love you, but please give me time."*

Their euphoria of love was in limbo, Allan was terrified to say more in case he tipped the delicate balance of Susan's thoughts, she felt as though her innocence of life had been violated by his story of a world she did not know existed, she was no longer a virgin of world affairs.

Dishes were left on the table, they went to bed, lay apart and Susan did not have one second of sleep, at dawn she looked over at Allan, he was dozing, she crept downstairs made the coffee, woke him with a kiss on his lips and said, *"I don't give a damn what or who you are I love you Allan Lambert, but we must talk."*

She crept into bed, snuggled up and they made up for their long time apart. Eventually, they dressed, ignored the dishes, made endless pots of coffee and talked until dusk.

*"I've been brainwashed all my life against the Jews by my father,"* Susan said, almost apologetically.

*"Susan, I've been brainwashed most of my life to be an Englishman,"* Allan countered.

*"So, what is the answer?"* Susan said with anguish in her voice.

*"Darling, I've been told I don't need to change anything, my documents say I'm Allan Lambert, an Englishman and I can stay that way."*

*"What about your family?"* Susan said.

*"They will possibly think I'm a traitor to my nationality and religion, but darling none of it was of my making and I don't think of myself as a German or a Jew, I hope when we eventually meet my family they will understand, if not, you are the most important thing in my life, so how does Mrs Lambert sound? Let's get married as soon as possible."*

Susan had endless questions and eventually she was exhausted but content and sealed the day's discussion by saying, *"Darling I love you more than ever, I feel that I'm now part of your life, but I have one request."*

Allan looked, wondering what was coming.

*"I'd like to meet your mother, I feel such compassion, I want to get to know her and hopefully develop a bond between us to make up for all she has suffered and maybe we could give her a grandson called 'Simon Weisman Lambert."*

*"You know Susan, I don't deserve you."*

*"I know that,"* Susan replied, giving him a kiss on the cheek.

# My Son The Enemy

His leave was wonderful, Susan and he made up for the long months apart, talked and planned a wedding, he became acquainted with her friends and regularly visited her father even though he had no idea who they were.

Returning to the army after his leave Allan was promoted to the rank of Captain and much to Susan's delight he was posted to nearby Bedford garrison as a Stores Training Officer which meant he could return home every evening. He had continued with his identity as Allan Lambert, a British Army officer and was blissfully happy, life would be perfect if only he could be reunited with his mother.

*"I have no idea, and want nothing to do with you or her ever again."*

Allan had done what he had vowed never to do, he had tried to contact his Aunt Sarah for news of his mother only to discover she was divorced and Uncle John refused to even speak to Allan or allow him in his house, his hatred for the Jews was as bitter as ever, he was a lonely old man who blamed them for his downfall.

The local Rabbi was more helpful, was delighted to meet Allan after so many years, gave him her new address, phone number at Matlock, and during their conversation he disclosed the sacrifice that Sarah had endured to save Allan from being returned to Berlin almost twenty years ago. The information made Allan hate his uncle more than ever but very humble and grateful towards his Aunt Sarah.

She was overjoyed to receive his phone call and ecstatic to meet Susan and him two weeks later at her cottage on the outskirts of Matlock.

Susan and Sarah became friends as soon as they met and during the next four hours and endless cups of coffee they updated each other with news. Allan apologised to his aunt for his attitude at their last meeting being unaware of her sacrifice on his behalf, and promised to make amends, however the most emotional point in the whole afternoon was when Sarah went to a cupboard and without comment quietly handed Allan a letter, it was written in German, she sat down and translated it out loud to Allan and Susan who sat together on the sofa holding hands with tears flowing throughout the translation.

The long letter was from Allan's mother, she was alive and well, being cared for by brother Albert and his wife, but longed to travel to England to see Sarah and hoped to contact her beloved son, she also disclosed that their parents had perished but said very little about her own treatment by the Nazis.

Allan, Susan and Sarah hatched a plot, in spite of his great urge to make immediate contact with his mother he agreed to remain quiet, allow Sarah to arrange for his mother to visit England on holiday, Allan and Susan would arrange the date for their wedding, to coincide with their visit. Allan and his mother would meet for the first time in almost twenty years on his wedding day.

My Son The Enemy

# Chapter Thirty Two
# A Meeting From Heaven

On May 10th 1949 Irene Weisman, her brother Albert and his wife Hannah arrived at their sister Sarah's home in Derbyshire for a proposed three month holiday.

The reunion was extremely emotional for them all, so much had happened since they had last been together seventeen years ago, Albert and Hannah had lost their beloved children, Irene had spent over six years as prisoner of the Germans and then the British, their father and mother had been murdered by the Nazis, and although she had survived the London bombings Sarah had sacrificed her happiness to ensure that Irene's son had been saved.

Sarah acted as interpreter being the only one able to speak English.

They spent hour after hour updating each other on the past seventeen years, Irene gave them a sketchy outline of her life in the Ghetto and the concentration camp, the emotion between Albert, his wife and two sisters was at times too hard to proceed, but they were aware that a line needed to be drawn on the past to allow them to begin a new life, even Albert gave a brief outline of his activities as a terrorist.

*"Now for some good news!"*

Sarah changed the mood of the conversation. They were now all aware of the life that Irene's son had lived since landing in England over seventeen years ago, Sarah had left nothing out, he was alive, that was all that mattered.

*"We are all invited to a wedding in two days time at Bedford, so tomorrow we go shopping and the next day will be a new beginning for all of us, our lives will start all over again."*

In spite of tears of pleading Sarah would not elaborate, she would not spoil the joy ahead in only forty hours time.

Sarah was financially secure, Albert was reasonably wealthy, still owned most of the jewels his father had given him many years ago, and he had already halved them with his sister. Consequently they arrived at the Grand Hotel in Bedford to three rooms already booked, and they were dressed to an elegance that Irene believed had passed her by. She had a pale blue dress with a picture hat to match, it seemed as if she was reborn, even her stoop and limp were less noticeable and an occasional smile flicked her lips.

Within half an hour of arrival at the hotel a huge bouquet of flowers was delivered to each room with an unsigned note which simply said, *"Enjoy the day."*

*"Please Sarah, tell me, whose wedding are we attending, will I be seeing Simon soon?"*

Irene's mind was in a whirl, she felt she could not handle much more, yet was elated to a height she had never experienced, life was suddenly overflowing, she only needed to meet Simon and she would explode with happiness. It took all of Sarah's willpower to refrain from telling Irene, but only three more hours of her restraint was required.

They arrived in a chauffeur driven limousine to a church that was already half full and they were directed to the front row at the groom's side, Sarah insisted that Irene was in the end seat near the aisle. Irene did not question the seating plan but was beginning to feel her heart thumping, there were so many uniforms in the congregation it was obvious this was no ordinary wedding and she had been manoeuvred into the prime seat.

The organ began to fill the church with a blanket of soothing music, the bridegroom and his best man walked to the front within six feet of Irene, Sarah suddenly took hold of her sister's hand like a vice, at the same time as Captain Allan Lambert, resplendent in his dress uniform, turned, knelt down to Irene, looked directly through his tear filled eyes and whispered, *"Hello mother."* (Sarah repeated his words in German for Irene to understand but it was unnecessary).

Only Allan's arm around her shoulder and Sarah's hold of her hand avoided her collapse, she could not breathe or speak, simply stared at this handsome young man who had declared he was her beloved son. Before she could respond the organ began *"Here comes the bride,"* Allan gave his mother a hug and a wonderful kiss on the cheek, she could only sit in a daze as everyone else stood for the entrance of the bride. As Susan reached Irene, she stopped, went over to her and with a hug and a long kiss on the cheek whispered, *"Hello, I'm going to be your daughter-in-law."*

Irene heard very little of the ceremony, she quietly sobbed with a happiness far beyond her belief, she could only sit and look at the back of her son, he was tall and erect just like his father, blonde hair like his father and his voice had the same lilt of her beloved husband.

Sarah held her hand tightly, Albert and Hannah were concerned but Irene was filled with contentment, she wished this moment could be never ending, her son was at the beginning of his life with the most beautiful girl she had ever seen.

Allan and Susan delayed their honeymoon for a week, Irene took to Susan immediately they met, and Allan insisted that everyone was introduced to his mother and other members of his family. Weddings are always happy occasions but Irene was convinced no wedding could surpass the wedding of her son.

They were booked into the Grand Hotel for a week, during which time they bridged the gap since Allan had been put on a train in Berlin at the age of five.

Although Irene had a twinge of sadness at her beloved Simon now being called Allan and no longer a practising Jew, she understood and accepted the situation, he was alive with a beautiful wife and they wanted her into their lives, nothing else mattered.

In a private conversation Allan and his uncle were reconciled and agreed to put the past behind them.

The end of their week's holiday arrived and with sadness their goodbyes were prolonged but with the clear understanding that no matter what the future had in store for them, they would always maintain contact.

Susan and Allan stood arm in arm as they waved goodbye to Irene, Albert and Hannah.

Silently Susan wished her father could have been at her wedding, but she had a husband, and a new mother-in-law who she simply adored.

Hopefully Allan and Susan's wedding would mark a new beginning for the Weisman family.

Their experience would never be forgotten, Irene lost her mother and father, had suffered unbelievable horror under the Nazis and due to the anti-semitic attitude of her brother-in-law, her dear son was more of an Englishman than the German Jew of his birth. However, he was alive and nothing else mattered, she was determined to get the most out of what life she had left, after all she was alive, unlike the millions of Jews who had died in barbaric circumstances, she would try to forget but would never ever forgive the Germans.

Although Albert believed that his acts of violence were justified in the cause of the new State of Israel, he hoped to forget for the sake of his own sanity but he would never forgive the Palestinians for killing his two little girls.

Palestinians who were forcibly removed from their homes to facilitate the creation of the new State of Israel could only join the exodus of thousands of their compatriots into exile, identical to the initial action taken by Germany against the Jews in the 1930s. Many may eventually forget, would they ever forgive the Jews?

Families of hundreds of British servicemen killed by Palestinians and Jews alike, accept that their loved ones were targets in the middle of a conflict. They may eventually forget the circumstances but cannot forgive.

Death, torture and violence was the background of life for the Weisman family from the early 1930s until the late 1940s. This is the story of only one family who are now a statistic among millions.

My Son The Enemy

# Epilogue

## Albert And Hannah Weisman

Returned to Israel, rekindled their love and Albert was involved in major political activities in order to maintain a permanent homeland for the Jews, no longer a man of violence he now hoped for a life of peace.

However, the Palestinians have a long memory and nine months after returning to Israel a Palestinian suicide bomber blew himself up killing twenty Jewish men, women and children, included in the carnage were Albert and Hannah Weisman ex residents of Berlin, Germany.

## Sarah

Never returned to Germany, she was quite content to live the life of a divorcee at Matlock in Derbyshire, her ex-husband John died four years after Allan's wedding, he didn't leave a will and as his only next of kin Sarah became a wealthy lady. She developed a high standard of excellence in watercolour painting, became involved in numerous activities in the community and maintained a close and constant contact with her sister Irene.

Sarah died at the age of 89 years old, had enjoyed her later years and passed on a small fortune to her nephew who she always called Simon. (His name, Allan Lambert reminded her too much of her husband).

# Irene

Never returned to Israel, extended her holiday with Sarah and applied for permanent residence which was accepted. She and Sarah enjoyed life to the full and on one jaunt in London Irene met Matthew a Jewish resident of New York, he was two years older than Irene, he'd never been married and was involved in the film industry, they were compatible from the moment they met, when he was in London they were inseparable, she occasionally visited New York, and they had a happy loving relationship without the trappings or commitment of marriage. Her base was in Derbyshire with Sarah and she was devastated when her sister died.

Her relationship with Allan and Susan was wonderful, particularly when they kept their promise and christened their first son 'Simon Weisman Lambert'. Their daughter was called Irene and although the name Weisman would not continue, Irene was living a happy and contented life than she ever contemplated during the dark days of the concentration camp.

Irene spent her final months in a nursing home near her son and died peacefully on her ninetieth birthday.

# Allan and Susan

Allan Lambert continued with the name given to him at the age of five years, he never acknowledged or practised the Jewish faith and considered himself as an Englishman, with an English name but void of any religious belief.

He had a successful army career and after thirty years service he'd attained the rank of Brigadier, and was awarded the D.S.O. for his service in Northern Ireland during the troubles. Now retired he'd launched on a new career as a writer with limited success, but he was a happy and contented man.

Susan and he had moved to a wonderful detached house in Surrey where his mother had regular visits prior to her moving into a specialist nursing home nearby. He and Susan had visited her every day, became incredibly close, and her death was both a relief from her suffering, but a moment of intense sadness.

Susan and he had a loving married life with a son and daughter they cherished, and awaiting grandchildren expanding the Lambert family.

*"Yes, Darling, I promise I will begin very soon."*

Allan was replying to Susan's constant plea for him to write the story of the Weisman family, who were based in Berlin in the 1930s.

# My Son The Enemy